THANKSGIVING DINNER DEATH
JUNIPER HOLIDAY COZY MYSTERY BOOK 2

LEIGHANN DOBBS

CHAPTER ONE

The Holiday mansion was currently a madhouse. Thanksgiving was the next day, and there were dozens of people in Juniper's kitchen, running around like chickens with their heads cut off in their haste to get everything ready in time. Naturally, Sabrina couldn't be expected to cook for hundreds of people on her own, so Juniper had called in Bite-Sized Catering to help out with the spread, and Sabrina was ordering them around like a general on the battlefield. Her mother would have been proud.

The savory aroma of roast turkey mingling with cinnamon and spices made Juniper's mouth water. Golden-crusted pies had been set on the table to cool, and the helpers were chopping and mixing to prepare some of the food ahead of time.

Up until a few minutes ago, Juniper herself had been helping, too, but she could sample the fare only so many times before she was ordered out. Which, honestly, was totally fine with her. She needed some fresh air anyway.

Before she could make it out the door, Jacobi, her ghostly cook, stopped her. "Why do you continue to let that woman butcher my family's recipes, Juniper Holiday? Do you know how long it took us to perfect them? Hmm?"

Juniper had to bite her tongue quickly in order to keep from saying the exact wrong thing, which would set Jacobi off. The last time she'd spoken without thinking very carefully about her words, he'd thrown a ghost-sized tantrum, and everyone had suffered for it. She still couldn't eat lemon meringue pie without tasting salt.

She cleared her throat. "A very long time?"

"Indeed," Jacobi affirmed, puffing his chest out with pride. "Every ingredient was carefully chosen in order to perfectly complement the dish." His bushy brows suddenly lowered over his ghostly eyes. "And that woman is ruining everything!"

Juniper sighed to herself. He had to be talking about the dressing. "Jac, honey, I'm sure Sabrina didn't mean to butcher the recipe," she said, "but you have to understand that she's under a lot of pressure right now. She's got dozens of people in her kitchen who don't know how she runs it, and you shouldn't blame her. Besides, you should at least try her improve—er, changes to your treasured recipes before you complain they're ruined. That's fair, ain't it?"

Jacobi continued to stare at her in ghostly anger, his form slowly bobbing up and down in front of her. Then, with a great sniff, he began to rise toward the ceiling, glaring at her the whole way—and there was a good fifteen feet to float—until he disappeared.

At least he didn't make the food explode, she thought, rubbing her temples.

Remembering her original plan, she scooted down the hall to the foot of the main staircase, taking time to admire the holiday décor as she went. She hadn't gotten too carried away because she planned to break out the Christmas decorations right after Thanksgiving, but she wanted the place to look festive for the dozens of guests who would arrive for the meal.

Displays of pumpkins were set about in various places. Big pumpkins, small pumpkins, orange pumpkins, white pumpkins. It was quite a display. The fireplace mantels had been draped in garlands of fall leaves in bright red, yellow, and orange, and colorful flower arrangements completed the look.

"Tori!" she yelled up the stairs, which had been draped in a fall-themed garland, "I'm going into town. You need anything?"

Three sets of feline eyes blinked back at her. The housecats, Loki, Luna, and Finn, had been banished from the kitchen and dining areas for the dinner. No one wanted cat hair in their gravy. The cats were quite annoyed at this, and Juniper could see the recrimination in their luminescent gazes. She knew she had better be on her guard, because she was sure they would find some unpleasant way to pay her back.

"What are you going for?" Tori yelled back.

"I've been banned from the kitchen."

"Ha! Bring me back a coffee and I'll love you forever."

"You've promised me that dozens of times already."

"And I'm promising it again. Make it sweet, Juni!" Tori warned. "Plain is nasty."

"All right," Juniper called back, shaking her head and rolling her eyes as she made her way out. Her dear goddaughter liked those sticky-sweet concoctions from WitchRoast Café, whereas Juniper preferred a bold, dark roast with a hint of cream and a touch of sugar.

At least Tori didn't like stump water, which was what Juniper called any coffee that wasn't so strong that a spoon could stand up in it on its own. She would have had to disown her for that.

Peeling out of the drive in her pretty little GT, the radio blasting "Killer Queen" by Queen, Juniper made the trip into town.

The smell of fall was heavy in the air, touched with a hint of winter waiting around the corner, and Juniper breathed it in as she got out of her car and headed into the warm, cozy interior of the cafe. The smell of coffee and pastries was strong as she stepped inside, and she nearly moaned at the delicious aroma.

"Hey, June!" Quincy Gilbert greeted her from behind the counter.

She raised her hand in a wave. "Hey, Quince."

"The usual?"

"Yep," she said with a nod. "And Tori wants something sweet, so maybe that unicorn-looking drink on the menu for her."

"You got it," he said with a chuckle.

Juniper moved to sit at one of the tables next to the window to wait. Not long after she'd sat down, a young woman with long dark hair took the seat across from her and slid something across the table to her.

"Put that on," the girl said, lifting her hand to reveal a small sterling silver ring fitted with a black stone.

Juniper raised her brow. "Why?"

"Because it will protect you," the girl said, her dark-blue eyes steady as she gazed directly into Juniper's.

Juniper raised her other brow. "Why do I need protection? And who the heck are you?"

The girl smiled. "You know at least one secret of the Cove, Juniper Holiday. That alone opens you up to tragedy and danger." She pushed the ring closer with the tip of her finger. "Put it on. You'll thank me for it later."

And then she was gone. No name. She just got up and left.

"She wasn't bothering you, was she?" Quincy asked as he came over with her drink order.

Juniper looked away from the window to peer up at him. "Who was that?"

"Her name's Halen," he said, his brows furrowed. "She's new to the Cove, but she's certainly memorable. She goes around offering protection charms and cryptic words of advice then leaves before anyone can get anything straight out of her." He shook his head. "I wouldn't take anything she told you to heart, June."

"No worries there," Juniper said, taking her drinks and standing.

"Oh, that's a nice ring. Where'd you get it?" Quincy asked.

Juniper frowned. She didn't remember putting on a ring. But when she looked at her hand, the ring Halen had pushed her way sat, pretty as you please, on her left pinky finger.

CHAPTER TWO

*E*verything was perfect.

Juniper Holiday stared down the long table in the center of the ballroom, her careful eye noting every detail, from the place settings to the name cards and even the cute little origami turkey decorations.

The seven tables she'd had set up in the dining room to accommodate all the guests were laden with silverware, fine china, and sparkling crystal glasses. Candles flickered in the centers of the tables, casting a warm glow over the gleaming surfaces.

Not one thing was out of order at any of the tables, including the one she had set up at the top of the room for special guests.

Her nose wrinkled at the idea of "special guests." As far as she was concerned, everyone she had invited was special. Well, almost everyone. Not that annoying Beatrice Miller, who lived up the road. Unless one considered her *specially* irritating. But there was a method to Juniper's madness. Beatrice was always calling the cops on her for being too loud, and she figured if she invited Beatrice to the dinner, then she wouldn't call the cops, and they could all eat in peace.

Speaking of annoying, this year, she had also extended an invitation to Crescent Cove's police force, detective Desmond Mallard, the D-Man himself, and his small crew of little officer ducklings. It was the least she could do since he'd made the effort to thank her for helping in the last case, even after her Halloween bash had been canceled—on his order, of course—due to murder.

If not for her and Tori covertly sussing things out, Desi the Duckman would never have figured out who had killed Hannah Peterson and then tried to store her body in a coffin meant for Juniper's Halloween haunted guesthouse. In the end, everything had worked out.

He'd caught the perp and then had even come by to let her know he was aware he couldn't have done it without their help.

Glancing at her watch, Juniper headed out of the ballroom. Five thirty. It was time to get dressed. She didn't want to be late for her own celebration!

Jacobi floated up to meet her halfway up the stairs, and she paused. "Did she do it? Were you able to convince her to spice up the sauce?"

It was a Thanksgiving tradition at the Holiday mansion to try a new recipe every year. This year, she had asked her cook to make a special sauce following one of Jacobi's old family recipes but with a little twist of her own, of course.

"No, madam. Sabrina, your corporeal cook, absolutely refuses to spike the punch," he said without even batting a ghostly eyelash.

"Spike the—?" Juniper narrowed her eyes. "Jacobi, I didn't request any such thing, and you know it." Her eyes suddenly widened. "Did you…?"

The man doubled over with laughter—an easy feat, given how transparent he was. "Your face! Oh my, Ms. Holiday, the look in your eyes was well worth that one, and your expression was totally priceless!"

"Yes, well, so is your grandmother's gravy boat. Or so it was. I believe one of the caterers dropped it this morning…"

"Ah, ah, ah," he tsked. "No, madam, I shall not fall for that one. Or, as you and Ms. Tori say, 'I absolutely am not buying it.' I was just in the kitchen myself, you see, and it's too early. They haven't yet begun to pour the sauces."

At the top of the stairs, Juniper paused again. "Well, they'd better get at it. Our guests will be arriving soon, and I expect every single detail to be perfect."

"Of course you do," he mumbled before nodding to indicate he would do his best to see that it was so. "By the way, lovely ring you're wearing, Ms. Holiday."

Juniper's brows snapped downward even as she brought her hand up to stare at the thing again. But rather than let on that she wasn't even aware she'd been wearing it or didn't know the girl who had given it to her from Adam's housecat, she said, "Isn't it, though? I think I'll keep it on through dinner as well. Wonder if I have anything at all in my wardrobe to match it."

Over her shoulder, she called back to her ghostly cook, "You should taste the sauce, Jacki, my boy. Sabrina did a good job with the enhancements, and I really think you'll enjoy it."

"Taste the…" Jacobi peered up at his mistress, a look of confusion on his face. "I don't think that would be such a great idea, Ms. Holiday, considering my current ethereal state and all."

Juniper whirled, a sparkle in her eyes that hadn't been there before. "Gotcha! I gotcha that time, Jac!"

Laughter trilling behind her as she rushed toward her room, Juniper called back again. "Woo-hoo-hoo! It's going to be great, Jacobi Wallach. I can feel it in my bones! Hey, make sure Tori is dressed and ready, will ya? It's almost six, and I don't want anyone to be late."

CHAPTER THREE

*D*esmond adjusted his tie in the oval mirror in the entryway before making his way into the ballroom. Dozens of people were milling about, each and every one of them a notable and influential citizen of the Cove. It astounded him that Juniper Holiday counted herself among them, if only because she was so very different from them. They were the country club type, and Desmond was willing to bet his favorite suit that Juniper hadn't stepped foot inside such a place in years, if ever.

She liked loud music of a specific type, drove a sporty little car that every teenager in Crescent Cove lusted after, and didn't seem to care what anyone thought of her.

Of course, she was also loud and opinionated and kept sticking her nose where it didn't belong—namely into his business. More specifically, his work. But he had to admit that she did have good instincts, and he'd even thanked her for her contribution to the last case, even though he really hadn't needed her assistance. Surprisingly, the acknowledgment had gotten him a personal invitation to Juniper's Thanksgiving celebration, which was his only reason for being here today.

Normally, he would have passed the day alone at home, having dinner for one. Looking over the crowd, he couldn't help but wonder if that was preferable to his current situation.

"Well, look at you, all spiffed up. Lookin' good, Desi."

He glanced to his right, where Victoria Cooper, Juniper's goddaughter, had slipped up behind him. His skin prickled with a rush of awareness that made him feel too warm. He nodded to her, his eyes sweeping over her soft form, which was clad in a slinky sky-blue dress that hugged her in all the right places. She was wearing her blond hair down, and her blue eyes looked brightly at him. "Ms. Cooper. You look—"

"Stunning. Ravishing. Gorgeous. Beautiful. I always liked it when a man told me I looked good enough to eat too," Juniper cut in before Tori could answer.

Desmond fought the sigh that rose to his lips and turned to greet his hostess. "Ms. Holiday."

Juniper grinned at him then gave him a thorough once-over, ending with a low whistle. "Goodness, D-Man. You clean up nice, if I do say so myself."

Desmond's brow rose slightly. "It's only a suit. You've both seen me in one plenty of times."

"Yeah, but this one is different," Juniper said, walking around him in a slow circle. "It makes you look…." She snapped her fingers. "Tori, what's the word I'm looking for?"

"Approachable? Handsome?" Tori offered, smiling at him in a way that made him feel flustered.

"Human! That's the word."

Tori snorted and took his arm before he could respond, pulling him away from her godmother. "Ignore her," she said. "You know how she is."

"Yes," he said curtly, tugging at his cuffs. "I do."

Tori laughed, the sound soft and sweet. "I probably shouldn't tell you this, but as ridiculous as it sounds, Juni only picks on you because she likes you."

A surprised laugh slipped from Desmond's mouth. "You'll have to forgive me, Ms. Cooper, but I can't believe that."

"It's true," Tori insisted. "Look around you. Do you see her doing that with anyone else?"

Desmond looked around until he spotted Juniper. She'd moved near the staircase and was engaged in conversation with Mayor Berkshaw and his wife, Susan. Her body language was no different than if she was talking to him or Victoria, and her smile seemed pleasant enough, but something was off. Desmond's brows dipped in a frown. She looked like a completely different person.

"See what I mean?" Tori asked.

For once in his life, words escaped him.

Laughing, Tori wrapped her arm around his and led him into the ballroom, where dinner was being served. "Come on, let's eat. You'll be better able to process what you've seen on a full stomach."

※

*J*uniper leaned back in her chair with a sigh and patted her stomach. "Welp, I'm stuffed. How 'bout y'all?" she asked, looking to her right and left at Desmond and Garrett, though her question was for everyone at her table. Along with Juni, the group comprised Desmond; Tori; their neighbor Fedora Layhee; her friend Garrett; his wife; and Tori's friend Trent.

The food had been divine. The turkey platter had been decimated, there was barely a spoonful of mashed potatoes left, and the stuffing had gone quicker than free snacks at an office party.

Judging by the satisfied looks on everyone's faces, the other diners agreed. This year's dinner had gone off without a hitch, and she was quite proud of her staff for making it happen. She would have to give them all a hefty surprise bonus, because they deserved it.

Jacobi and Felicity floated above the living guests. Jacobi looked on with only slight disapproval because there had been several raving compliments to the chef over the dressing and specially modified sauce. Lissy was grinning ear to ear at the sight of everyone having a good time. Lionel was probably elsewhere because he took his job as butler quite seriously despite being deceased.

After some time had passed to allow for everyone's food to digest a bit more, coffee was brought out to signal the end of the meal.

Juniper had an extensive collection of expensive coffee cups, each of them gold-dipped on the inside and with a different flower decoration on the outside. Juniper had a favorite with pansies on it, so when one of the extra staff placed a cup with roses on it before her, she handed it back.

"Oh, no, dear. I always drink from the cup with the pansies. Could you bring that one?" The girl whisked the rose-covered cup away, and Juniper witnessed some whisperings over at the coffee urn between her and another helper. So what if they thought the request was a bit precious? Juniper was known to be eccentric, and she liked it that way.

The other waitstaff woman looked familiar. Was that Beatrice Miller's long-suffering maid? Juniper glanced around the room, wondering if Beatrice knew her maid was moonlighting. The poor girl would probably get fired.

Juniper fiddled with the ring on her pinky absentmindedly as she participated in the conversation around her.

"You've been messing with that thing all evening," Desmond remarked out of the blue. "Is it loose?"

"Hardly," Juniper said with a snort. "It fits surprisingly well, actually." She wiggled her pinky at him to demonstrate—and the ring promptly slipped off her finger and plopped into the cup of coffee that had just been placed in front of her. Juniper stared at it with her mouth open.

"You were saying?" Desmond asked drolly.

Before she could say anything, he took her cup and fished around in the warm brew for a second before pulling the ring out. He placed it on the napkin next to her plate.

"I believe this belongs to you."

Juniper snorted and shook her head. "And that coffee now belongs to you, Waddlebutt, since you had your fingers in it."

She didn't really expect him to drink the coffee, but that was exactly what he did. In a move that surprised even her, Desmond Mallard, pain in her tail, looked right in her eyes and drank her coffee in one go.

Juniper cackled.

Desmond grimaced and smacked his lips. "That is one bitter brew, Ms. Holiday."

Before Juniper could rib him about his coffee tolerance, Desmond's expression morphed into a horrible grimace.

"Gah!" he said.

And then he face-planted in his pecan pie.

The room went deathly quiet as all eyes turned toward them. Juniper stared at Desmond's prone form in disbelief. The coffee wasn't *that* bad.

"Juni?" Tori asked, looking down the table, her brows drawn in concern. "Is he okay?"

"I don't know," she answered. She shook him. No response. She frowned. "Desmond Mallard, you better not be trying to mess with me now, you twerp," she said, poking him in the side.

He didn't react.

Juniper's stomach suddenly felt as if it was full of ice water. She put her fingers to his neck and felt all the blood drain from her face.

She looked at Tori. "He's… I think he's dead, Tor."

CHAPTER FOUR

"9:17," Juniper heard Garrett mumble as he jumped up from his chair, taking immediate charge of the situation. He came around her and put two fingers on Desmond's neck. "Nah, his pulse is just faint, I think. Juniper, your car's faster than any of the ambulances from Cove General. Bring it around. The rest of you stay calm. Juniper and I will get him to the best of care."

Without waiting for permission or assistance, Garrett hefted Detective Mallard over his shoulder and started for the door.

"I'll grab my purse," Juniper called after him. "I'll meet you at the car."

A few moments later, she slid into the driver's seat. "What are you playing at, Gar? And why was the time significant enough for you to whisper it in my ear? That man is stone-cold dead, and we both know it!"

She stuffed the key into the ignition, slung the shifter into reverse, and peeled out of the driveway.

Garrett didn't even reach for the grab handle. Instead, he glanced back over his shoulder to make sure they weren't being followed. "We know it, Juni, but they don't, and right now, that's all that matters. As for the time, Quincy needed it to know what to prepare."

Ignoring his mention of the cafe owner, Juniper railed, "But you said to take him to the hospital! As soon as we take him there, they're going to pronounce him dead! Good grief, I've had about enough of dead bodies *and* of Detective Mallard, I tell you. Enough to last me a lifetime! Maybe two!"

"We *will* take him to the hospital, but your speed-demon habits should buy us just enough time to get him the help he needs before the ER can get their hands on him," Garrett told her.

"Oh, so you werewolves know people who

can bring back the dead? Is that it?" Juniper shook her head. "I may drive like a NASCAR wannabe, Garrett, but his little duck boys aren't going to let him out of their sights for long. We have probably three minutes before they come screaming up beside us, sirens blaring."

"We only need two," Garrett assured her. "Less if my text to Quincy went through."

He looked at his phone just as Juniper's eyes went wide. "Oh no! You texted Quincy about the detective? Garrett, how stupid can you get? Dude, the police are gonna call that grounds to arrest you as an accessory to murder, you numbskull! I thought I knew you better than that."

His smirk was anything but reassuring. "Juni, Juni, Juni-june. You do, girl. You do. I texted codes, sweetheart. He doesn't know everything, but he knows what most likely happened, so he will know exactly what to meet us with."

"Meet us? At the hospital? Garrett, you're just bringing more people in, and I don't want to be responsible for all this mess, I tell ya."

"You won't be. He's not meeting us at the ER. We are meeting him at WitchRoast Café. Like, now. Turn now, Juni!"

She did, which caused the tires to screech

again. Not that anyone noticed or cared. The second anyone in the Cove recognized Juni's car, the sound of tires screeching would have been nothing out of the norm. She hit the brakes right at the cafe door, just like Garrett told her to. "Where is he?"

Quincy flung the door open and rushed to the back of the car. Garrett jumped out to help.

"Hold him, Garrett. Now, let's get this down him," he said, upending a little brown bottle over Desmond's lips. After the liquid was in the detective's mouth, well, Quincy did what he had to do to make the dead man swallow.

"There. You have about six minutes to get him into the ER before that takes effect, and your dead man will be walking again—provided he ingested the type of poison we think he did. If not—" He spread his hands wide. "I may be a warlock and a grand potions master, but my powers of persuasion lie on this side of the great divide."

Garrett clapped him on the back in a gesture of thanks. "Good job, man. I'll let you know how things work out."

He slid back into the car and closed the

door, and Juniper hit the gas again, her eyes glued to the rearview mirror to see Quincy waving goodbye as they hit the highway once more.

"Six minutes?" she asked. "Why so long? We will have him in the hospital ER in less than five."

Garrett shrugged. "Maybe the guy is smarter than we know. You did pronounce Detective Mallard's death. The ER will confirm it. Then they will also witness his miraculous recovery firsthand."

"Will the techs be able to trace whatever Quincy made him swallow?" Juniper asked, feeling nervous again.

"Not if I know Quincy." He grinned. "And I do. Nothing gets by that man, Juni. Absolutely nothing."

A couple of minutes later, they pulled into the covered ER drive, and Garrett rushed in to get a stretcher and an orderly. Both of Juniper's hands gripped the furry pink steering-wheel cover while she waited for news that the nosy detective her goddaughter especially liked had finally managed to revive.

A horrible thought crossed her mind—what if Garrett was wrong? What if Quincy hadn't gotten his spells and potions right? What would she tell Tori when all this was over? That it was her fault the dastardly Duckman had died?

"Can you step out of the car, please, Ms. Holiday? Step out of the car and put your hands on the trunk," said a voice outside the driver's-side window.

Juniper glanced over and saw one of Desmond's little ducklings on the other side of her car door. She reached for the keys with one hand and her purse with the other. If the D-Man was going to resurrect, he oughta do it pretty soon, Juniper decided. She might as well wait for the news outside.

"No, no. Leave the keys. Leave your purse. Leave everything but yourself inside," Mr. Quackers told her.

Juniper did as he said, although if he had been a wise officer of the law, he would have asked her to holster her most dangerous weapon—her mouth—which she immediately began to exercise. "Look here, Mr. Flannerman, or whatever your badge says. The detective is sick. He needs a doctor. My friend has already taken him inside."

The junior detective nodded. "Yes, ma'am. I know. But Detective Mallard was pronounced dead on arrival, and you're our chief suspect. We have orders to take you in, Ms. Holiday, for the murder of Desmond Mallard."

CHAPTER FIVE

*D*esmond felt... off. He couldn't exactly explain how; it was more that he just felt... different. Kind of fuzzy around the edges. Lighter. He almost felt as if he was floating, to be honest. But that was ridiculous. He couldn't be floating. Gravity was a thing he believed in very much.

Everything was blue too. Not a harsh blue. Not baby blue. Just... blue. And fuzzy. Or was it fluffy? It might be fluffy, because it made him think of cotton candy.

Flavor burst on his tongue, as if thinking the words "cotton candy" had conjured the taste in his mouth.

This was very *odd*.

Bit by bit, the oddness began to wear off, and he became aware of more than just the color blue, the taste of cotton candy, and the feel of fluffiness. Sound began to leech in, soft at first then more robust. It was loud. People were talking, almost yelling back and forth to one another. They did not seem angry, though. More…direct, would be the word, he supposed.

There were beeping noises. They almost sounded like a heartbeat. How strange.

He was awfully cold. Or was he hot? He… burned. Or did he sting? Like thousands of ants biting him at once. He could feel it in his blood.

Why?

Sharp white light stung his eyes, first one then the other. "Mr. Mallard. Mr. Mallard, blink if you can hear me."

Yes, he could hear them, whoever they were. They were awfully loud. He blinked.

More chattering.

The feeling of being moved.

Where was he?

He tried to sit up, but his body would not obey, choosing instead to lurch and sway on the moving thing. He felt hands on him, pushing him flat again, and he groaned. His stomach was suddenly roiling.

Without warning, he turned onto his side and vomited. As soon as his stomach was emptied, he felt pain coursing through his body. He felt as if he'd run a marathon, swum a thousand leagues, and been crushed beneath a steamroller all at once.

What had that woman done to him? he wondered.

"What woman?" a voice asked.

"Juniper… Holiday," he mumbled and promptly passed out.

❧

*A*cross town, sitting in a holding cell, Juniper Holiday drummed her fingers on her cheek over and over again as she glared through the bars at Officer Big Britches. The skinny little dude was stronger than he looked, blast him. If he hadn't been, she would've been a free woman half an hour ago. Unfortunately, he had proved to have iron bands for hands, and so here she sat, still in her Thanksgiving dinner finery.

She sighed. "You're going to be wishing you'd let me out a long time ago when you find out your boss is still alive, you know. All the embarrassment coulda been avoided had you just listened to me instead of jumping to conclusions, but noooo. You had to be a big shot." At least she hoped Mallard was alive. Shouldn't the hospital have alerted them to the fact that he'd made a comeback already? What if the potion hadn't worked and he'd stayed dead?

Ackers leaned his head back and sighed before turning as if he was about to say something.

"*Don't* say a word," Haverman interceded. "She's just trying to get a rise out of you, man. Just ignore her. Believe you me, she'll be the one singing a different tune come morning."

"Yeah, but it ain't gonna be what you boys think!" Juniper said.

"What have you done with my godmother?"

Juniper leapt to her feet at the sound of Tori's voice, a giant grin on her face. "Tori-bori!"

Ackers and Haverman both glared over their shoulders at her.

Juniper raised her eyebrow and said, "What? Did you think I was going to call a lawyer? Pbbt! I'm innocent!"

Turning away from her, Ackers gave his full attention to Tori. "Ms. Cooper," he greeted her, his cheeks turning pink. "How can I help you?"

"You can start by releasing my godmother," Tori said, glaring at him as she smacked her purse down on the desk. "She's done nothing wrong."

Haverman cleared his throat and puffed out his chest. "Now, Ms. Cooper, you saw what happened back at the Thanksgiving dinner. She—"

"Obviously let Detective Mallard taste the devil's brew she calls coffee. Anybody would've passed out if they'd tasted her cup. She likes it so strong it'll knock a horse on its rear end."

"She said he was *dead*, Ms. Cooper," Haverman insisted.

Tori didn't back down. "Did you confirm his death, Officer? No? I didn't think so. What you saw—what we *all* saw—was Desmond Mallard face-plant in his dessert and Juni and Garrett haul butt to get him taken care of. Smelling salts probably would have worked just fine to get the detective back on his feet."

"Psst! Tori! Come here!" Juniper hissed in a stage whisper.

The look Victoria gave her could've melted the bars she was holding; it was that formidable. But Juniper wasn't fazed, waving her over like a teenaged girl getting her friend's attention.

Sliding a warning look at both police officers, Tori walked over to Juniper. Putting her face close to the bars, she hissed, "*What?*"

"They're not gonna let me go till they see Desmond Mallard alive and well for themselves, so you gotta do me a favor, Tortellini. You've got to go to the hospital and make sure he's still kicking."

Tori frowned. "I don't know how strong that coffee was, June, but surely it wasn't that bad."

Juniper gave her *a look*. "He really was dead," she mouthed.

Tori took a moment to decipher her lip movements, her eyes widening when she did, only to narrow back down to slits a second later. "You've got a lot of explaining to do when you get home," she muttered so only Juniper could hear her.

"And I will tell you everything when that happens, but for now, get your butt to that hospital, girl!"

CHAPTER SIX

*C*rescent Cove General Hospital was no different from any other she'd been in for one reason or another over the years. They all gave Victoria the creeps. Sick people, broken people—and, if Juniper had been telling it straight when she'd whispered through the bars of her jail cell earlier, dead people too—were often in residence in hospitals. Those were the top reasons she was careful to make sure she ate right, exercised daily, and basically took good care of herself. If it could be avoided, she never wanted to be a patient in a hospital anywhere.

Desmond, however. Poor guy. He'd had no choice in the matter, kicking over like he had. Where else could they have taken him?

Nowhere that she knew of. But it didn't make her like having to be there herself any better just because he was in their care.

At the nurses' station, she told the head nurse her name and who she was there to see. She was surprised to find he'd been placed in a triage bed for a few hours' monitoring and would be allowed to go home soon if everything turned out well.

"Can he have visitors? I'd like to see him if I may," she told the nurse.

"Yes, of course you can, but you'll have to wait for a bit. There's someone in there with him now."

Victoria scrunched her face up in a frown, but she nodded and turned toward the waiting room, which was set up like an entertainment lounge. There were chairs, a television, and several magazines as well as stacks of different varieties of medical literature for people to browse. "I'll just wait here, then."

She didn't wait long. Less than five minutes later, Garrett came walking into the waiting area, his expression kind of grim. "Hey! Garrett! You were back there with Detective

Mallard? What happened? How's he doing? Are they letting him out tonight?"

Garrett nodded while directing her toward the far side of the lounge area. "I was with him. He flatlined, but he's fine. Yes. He has another hour on the machines and a routine round with the docs, but he should be able to rest in his own bed tonight."

"Juniper said he really was dead!" Victoria leaned close to whisper. "How much can you tell me about that?"

His gaze guarded now, he said, "It's true. He was gone for more than five minutes. Nearly ten. But thanks to Quincy over at the WitchRoast knowing his potions, June's Duckmaster is alive and well and will be roasting her ass over his particular brand of fire before she can catch her breath now that he's found out what happened."

"What did happen, Garrett? Nobody has been able to clue me in so far, and I've got Juniper breathing down my neck from her jail cell, insisting she's innocent and they have to let her out of there." She cast a glance heavenward. "I'm here to talk to Detective Mallard and get clear cell phone footage proving he's exactly as well as she says he is so her jailers will let her out of her cage, as she calls it."

Garrett shot a quick glance around the empty lounge but still kept his voice low in case there were others in the vicinity with hearing as keen as his. "Poison, Tori. There was poison in that coffee Desmond sucked down. I'm sure it was meant for Juniper. It was her cup, after all. What I can't figure out is why."

Victoria's eyes went wide. "Someone tried to kill my godmother? Oh, dear lord, but why? Who would want to harm Juniper, Garry? And with poison—!" She shook her head in disgust.

"I know. Both cowardly and vile." He sighed and slipped his hands into his pockets. "I don't know the answers, Tor, but I'm sure June is gonna want to find out."

"The sooner the better," Victoria agreed, nodding. "I really do have to get her out of there. Somehow."

He laughed. "You'll figure it out, I'm sure, but right now, you'd better get yourself back there with the detective before they lock the doors. Visiting hours are done in half an hour."

Victoria's gaze shot toward the head nurse. "Hmm, yes, and I'm sure she wouldn't have a hard time rushing everyone out once the bell tolls. Thanks, Garrett. For everything you did, though I don't know what that was, either. I'll call you when we are home—provided I manage to get Juniper out."

"Ha! I'll bet she will be calling me if you don't. She doesn't give up, that one. Got a mouth like a drunken sailor at times, but her eyes miss nothing, and her brain is razor sharp."

Victoria's snort said without words how well she knew what he was saying to be true. "Yep! That's my godmother, all right!"

🌰

🌰

*D*esmond did his best to straighten up when Victoria Cooper walked into the curtained-off triage area. "Victoria. Why are you here? Shouldn't you be back at the mansion, handling Ms. Holiday's guests now that she's in jail for my murder?"

Tori slipped her purse under her arm. "I came to be sure you're okay, Desmond. Are you? That was some face-plant back there. You sure you're all right?"

He peered at her for a long moment before nodding. "I think so, yes, but I have no way of knowing for sure. You see, I've just been poisoned, Victoria. Would you know anything about that?"

She hurried to the bed and leaned close. "I know the coffee was intended for Juniper. You *died* for her, Desmond. Yes, I know about that. Can you imagine? She's going to *hate* that!"

There was a flash of amusement in her eyes, he noticed, but now he couldn't quite meet her gaze because, though he knew what she was saying, he also knew Juniper Holiday had been instrumental in saving his life. And his greatest fear at the moment was that she would find a way to use that information against him.

"Victoria, I think I am ready to go home. Can you drive me back to the precinct once I manage to get out of here?"

"Of course. Just let me know what you need. But first, I need to ask a favor." She screwed up her face in an apologetic little wriggle.

He stared at her. "A favor. Really."

She nodded. "Yes. You see, the guys at the

jail or department or whatever you guys call it haven't been notified that you aren't dead. They're holding Juniper on suspicion of your murder. I think they need to see your living, breathing self with their very own eyes. Video will work. I just need to get my phone. Will you do it?"

His sigh was filled with resigned exasperation. "Just do it, but quickly. The doctor will be around soon, and I don't want him to think I'm into taking selfies with lovely young women."

Victoria's laughter played surprisingly well on something in his insides. "Wow, they must have given you some powerful juju medication, Detective, 'cause right now, you're acting as silly as June does!"

His eyes narrowed, and he crossed his arms over his chest to complete the look. "Really, Victoria. Wow."

CHAPTER SEVEN

*J*uniper sat slumped in one of the overstuffed chairs in the informal living room. This room was tucked at the back of the mansion and was off-limits to everyone but the live-in staff, herself, Tori, and the animals. The cats had been aloof at first, but now, Finn was curled up in Juniper's lap, purring away as she stroked his silver fur. Loki was sprawled against Juniper's shoulder on the back of the sofa, his fluffy black tail swishing back and forth, and Luna was hiding under the sofa.

Barclay, Tori's beloved Jack Russell–Chihuahua mix, tended to stay with Tori in her room except when he was chasing the cats.

Juniper stared into the leaping flames in the

fireplace, her eyes narrowed as she petted Finn methodically.

It had been a couple of days since her stint in the local jail, and she was still miffed about the whole ordeal. Tori said she was being crotchety. Juniper insisted she was merely exercising her right to be angry at having been wrongfully detained. The only bright spot during the whole thing had been watching Mallard's ducklings chew their tongues when they had to let her go because, miracle of miracles, their boss was alive and well.

However, she was still a person of interest given how she and the detective had butted heads on more than one occasion—apparently, not getting along with someone automatically gave them motive to commit murder—and she would be until the case was solved or they found someone who disliked Desmond more than she did. Not to mention he had been poisoned by drinking her coffee.

But what irked her, *really* irked her, was the fact that apparently, the poisonous brew had been intended for her, which meant someone had it out for her. The question was: Who?

Who disliked her so much they wanted her

dead? Had tried to kill her, in fact! In her own house! With her favorite beverage! In her favorite cup! During one of her favorite holidays!

Gah! What was the world coming to?

"All right, Juniper, you've gotta snap out of this."

At the sound of Tori's voice, she sank lower in the chair, a ferocious scowl blooming on her face. "When you've been through what I've been through the past few days, Tori-bori, *then* you can tell me to get over it, but not a second before then."

"I didn't tell you to get over it," Tori said, plopping down in the chair next to Juniper. "I said you gotta snap out of it. You being in a funk is like Jack Nicholson's character in *The Witches of Eastwick* in the scene where the girls are gone and he's watching the tape they made. Terrifying."

Juniper cut her eyes at Tori in warning.

Tori simply pointed her finger at her. "See? You're doing it now. Stop."

Juniper huffed. "Well, what else am I supposed to do? Somebody tried to murder me, Victoria! Me! Juniper Holiday! For no reason!

But they botched it! Now I'm suspect numero uno in the attempted murder of one Detective Waddlebutt Desmond Mallard! Wouldn't you be a little angry?"

The look Tori shot her said this was anything but little.

"If you're trying to make me feel better, don't. It won't work, anyway. I. Am. Pissed."

"You. Are. Dramatic," Tori countered. "But I get it. You have every right to be angry. I would be. But you can't let someone's botched attempt at murdering you get you down."

Juniper snorted.

"I'm not joking. The Juniper I know would have started trying to connect the dots the second she got cuffed, if not before that."

Juniper didn't respond, knowing she would have done exactly that had she been thinking straight. But she didn't want to admit that she hadn't been. Of course, her one thought at the time had been to make sure Desmond didn't die on her. She didn't want to imagine where she would be if Quincy hadn't been there with his magic potion or Garrett with his quick thinking and fast acting.

She sighed, her scowl easing somewhat. "Fine. Where do you suggest we start?"

"Heck if I know."

Juniper growled, her scowl returning. "You're the one who writes all the murder mystery gothic romances! You don't have *any* ideas?"

"I make up everything as I go!" Tori defended herself. "I don't know anything before it happens! Usually…" she amended.

Juniper huffed again. Tired of her shoulders constantly moving and disrupting her sleep, Loki got down, choosing to curl up beside Tori instead.

"I suppose we need to look at who would want to kill you and who would have had access to your coffee," Tori said.

Juniper frowned. "Certainly none of our staff would want to kill me."

"Of course not; you treat them very well. But don't forget, we had hired extra help."

"Why would they want to poison me? They don't even know me. And who would have known to put it in that exact cup?"

Tori stared hard at her. "Someone who knows you always use that cup, or maybe the server knew which cup to give you. It could have been someone at the table… did anyone touch your cup?"

Juniper thought back, but she'd been busy chatting and had no idea. "The ring fell into it. That's how Duckman ended up drinking it."

"I suppose the police have both the cup and the ring. Anna did mention something about them taking the cup. She was very worried they wouldn't return it, and she'd have an incomplete service." Anna, the housekeeper, was very diligent about keeping the china and silver services intact.

Juniper half expected the mysterious ring to appear on her finger, but it didn't.

"I think we should look over the guest list. See if there was anyone invited who might have had it out for you. If that leads nowhere, look to the poison. See if Quincy can help figure out what kind it was and where it came from. Being the potions master he is and obviously knowing the antidote without having to have too much information, I'll bet he can point you in the direction you need to go."

"Yes, yes," Juniper said with a wave of her

hand. "You're not telling me anything I don't already know."

Tori smiled. "Then why are you moping about instead of trying to find out who did it?"

"Shut up."

Tori laughed. "All right, I'll get out of your hair, but only if you promise me you will actually look into things. It's weird when you're not you."

Juniper made a vague noise of assent and fluttered her hands about to get Tori to leave, which she did, shaking her head and talking to herself on the way.

Alone once more, save for the cats, Juniper's thoughts turned in a different direction. Whether she wanted to admit it or not, she needed Tori to make her get out of her head this time and approach the problem from a different angle.

Snapping to attention, she scooted Finn onto the cushion as she got up and headed out of the room, calling out as she went, "Tori! Where did I put that guest list?"

If her would-be murderer thought they'd gotten away with it, well, they had another think coming!

CHAPTER EIGHT

*H*ours later, Juniper stalked into Tori's writing area, dropped into a chair, and plopped the guest list she'd brought with her onto a table beside her. "It couldn't have been Fedora, could it? I mean, she was sitting right beside the Duckman. Maybe she poured something in my cup and used the seating arrangements for plausible deniability."

Tori gave her a look. "As ridiculous as it sounds, the detectives must have thought the same thing, because they picked up Fedora this morning for questioning."

Juniper's eyes widened. "Really? They took Fedora down to the station, and I wasn't around to see it?" Her palm smacked her forehead. "No wonder you insisted I get myself out of a funk! Wow. That must have been a sight."

"Not a pretty one," Tori told her. "Fedora was doing you proud, railing against the government machine, denying her part in anything, and insisting the detectives taking her away from her home against her will was going to earn them a solid count of kidnapping."

"Ha ha!" Juniper cackled and slapped her thigh. "That's my girl, Dorie. Don't let 'em get the upper hand!"

Tori's snort was anything but commiserating. "Are you forgetting you just came in here to ask if I thought she was the one who tried to murder you?"

"Yeah, you're right." Juniper straightened in the chair. "There's no telling what the baby ducks will decide. But why would Fedora want to kill me?"

"Good point," Tori said, though she wasn't really paying her godmother much attention.

Between each random bout of wordage Juniper spouted, Tori typed a few of her own into the story she was working on, a covert action Juniper finally noticed. She narrowed her eyes. "I can see you're not going to be a bit of help, so I might as well have asked the cats."

"Or the ghosts," Tori suggested, sarcasm heavy in her tone. "Look, I'm sorry, June, but I am really busy tonight."

"Fine, fine," Juniper told her as she gathered up the guest list once more. "I'll ask the ghosts and the living staff too. There's bound to be someone who has better ideas than you or me."

"For what it's worth," Tori called after her as she left the room, "my money's on the lady up the street who calls the cops on us every night. You know, that old bag who doesn't like your music and calls it all obscene racket and noise? I forget her name, but she was invited to Thanksgiving dinner. Maybe she slipped by your table and decided to top up your glass. Or, er, cup. Sorry."

"Beatrice Miller? That old goat?" Juniper waved away the suggestion. "She doesn't have the gumption, though I'm sure she wishes she had. Get to work, Tor-Tor. Finish your story. I'll see you tomorrow. I'm sure you'll be writing on it until long after I'm in bed tonight."

"I'll do that," Tori mumbled without looking up from the monitor.

Word after word appeared on her screen, and soon, she was lost again in the plot. She never noticed when Anna slipped into the room to place a throw over the chair in which she'd once again fallen asleep and then quietly dim the lights. She also would never know that Lionel himself stood at the door for the rest of the evening to ensure no one disturbed her rest.

※

Upstairs in her own room, Juniper cross-referenced the guest list with the diagram of the seating arrangements and came up with the same three names: Garrett to her right, Mallard right beside her, and Fedora to his left. The only others at the table were Garrett's wife and Tori's friend Trent, but the T-man absolutely adored her. Like Fedora and Garrett, neither of them had anything against her. They'd never try to hurt her, much less straight-up kill her —with poison or by any other means.

Could it have been one of the hired servers? But who and why?

She needed to find out more about the lethal

substance in her drink. Maybe once she did, that would give her a clue as to who would have access to that type of poison.

Snapping her fingers, she hopped off the bed and reached for her phone. While she couldn't very well accuse him herself, there was nothing stopping Garrett and Fedora. Her call to Garrett got her Garrett's wife. "They picked him up after dinner, Juniper."

"They picked up Garrett too? This morning, it was Fedora! What I cannot fathom, given how close both of them are to me, is why. Don't they know either of those two and myself, we would die for each other?"

"I don't know, Juni. All I know is that he told me not to worry when they cuffed him and stuck him in the back of their car. I laughed, of course, knowing what they don't know about Garry. I just hope they let him go soon, or they might force him to let them in on our little secret, if you know what I mean."

Juniper did. She and Tori had discovered Garrett's secret of being a werewolf one night that past summer when they'd had a hankering to go skinny-dipping in the lake at midnight. But they were among the few who knew that closely guarded bit of information.

Her mind flashed back to the strange woman, Halen, who had given her the ring. She'd said that Juni knew more than one Crescent Cove secret and needed to be protected. Did the woman know something about who had poisoned her?

She spent a few minutes sympathizing with Garrett's wife and then hung up the phone and walked to the big floor-to-ceiling windows in her bedroom. She pulled back the heavy drapes to look out over the clear, moonless night. Someone had honest to God tried to kill her. The authorities were barking up the wrong trees by suspecting her friends. Some weirdo in the cafe had slipped her a ring that had forced her to wear it on its own.

A snowflake smacked into her window, quickly followed by another. Soon, hundreds of the lovely geometric crystals were falling from the sky—not an unusual occurrence given that Christmas was just around the corner. But something smelled foul in Crescent Cove, and Juniper decided right then and there that Tori was right. She was Juniper Holiday, by whoever cared, and she would not let up until she figured out what it was.

Letting the curtain fall to cover the comforting scene before her, she turned on her heel and marched to the door for a second time. She was going out again, but this time, she was not headed to one of her usual haunts. It was time to put together a plan.

CHAPTER NINE

On the other side of town, sitting in the darkness of his office, Desmond pondered a legion of questions, each of them leading him right back to where he'd started: Who wanted Juniper Holiday dead?

He wasn't so arrogant as to think she had intended him to drink the turpentine she claimed was coffee. He shuddered at just the memory of that foul brew filling his mouth. He wasn't even sure what had possessed him to drink it—maybe a desire to prove Juniper wrong. It had been totally out of character, and he'd felt as if he was being compelled to gulp it down against his own common sense. He'd never tasted coffee so bitter in his life. But if

Juniper wanted him dead, she would have chosen a different method. Poison might have been a woman's weapon, but she wasn't one to go that route. He let himself smile at the thought of what method she might choose to off him.

She'd probably run him over with her car.

The longer he sat there, trying to unravel the threads that would lead him to Juniper's intended killer, the more his head began to pound until he couldn't make heads or tails of his own thoughts. He needed to either call it quits for the night or call in reinforcements. A quick glance at his watch showed the time was barely past ten. He'd worked longer nights on less information. He wasn't about to give up on this one so quickly, so reinforcements it was.

Reaching for his phone, he called Ackers then Haverman and asked them to come down to the precinct. As he waited for them to arrive, he dragged a whiteboard into the biggest, emptiest room they had and wrote down the information they already knew, as well as possibilities that could lead somewhere if the threads proved worth picking up.

When he was done, he checked the time

again, aggravated to see that not nearly enough time had passed for his men to arrive, so he went into the breakroom and put on a pot of *decent* coffee. He'd just poured himself a cup and added a splash of creamer when he heard Haverman call out, asking his whereabouts.

Stepping out of the breakroom, Desmond raised his cup. "I'm here. There's coffee if you want it."

Haverman didn't answer verbally, just made a beeline for the door. Desmond figured he needed it. The poor guy looked like he'd just nodded off. But that was part of the job; they were always on call. People weren't saved while they were asleep.

Ackers showed up a few minutes after Haverman, looking chipper and eager to get down to business. Desmond wondered if maybe it hadn't been a mistake calling him in, given the state both he and Haverman were in. There was only so much joy a sleep-deprived person could take and not revolt.

After everyone had caffeine in them, Desmond proceeded to walk them through everything he'd already gone through in his head, which he'd drawn out on the whiteboard.

He ended with, "There's something that has gotten overlooked every time, however. A crucial point in this case that proves Juniper Holiday is not a suspect."

Immediately, Haverman and Ackers jumped in with why they disagreed. It was common knowledge that she and he were like two negative sides of magnets, constantly repelling one another. Desmond couldn't deny that, but neither could he deny the fact that Juniper had saved his life, whether he liked it or not. He was forever indebted to her, and he wasn't about to forget it.

"It was Juniper's cup I drank from."

"Yeah, Boss, we know. She must have poisoned it when you weren't looking."

Desmond sighed. "No. You're not hearing what I'm saying. It was *Juniper's* cup I drank from."

Ackers and Haverman shared a look that clearly said they thought their boss was losing it. Looking back at Desmond, Ackers said, dragging the word out, "Yeeeaaahh, we know."

Desmond felt his eyes narrow. "Clearly, you are not connecting the dots."

"There don't seem to me to be that many

dots to connect, Boss," Ackers said. "Everybody knows she doesn't like you much. Honestly, we're surprised she didn't try to kill you last month when you pulled the plug on her Halloween bash."

Desmond pressed his lips together and reined in his irritation. At the moment, he was having a hard time remembering why he had chosen these numbskulls to be on his team.

Breathing in through his nose, he closed his eyes and counted down from twenty. When he felt more in control, he said, very calmly, "Listen to me closely, both of you, because I'm only going to explain this once. The cup I drank from that contained the poison that almost ended my life was Juniper's." He held his hand up when it looked as if Haverman would interrupt. "Think about it. The poison was already in the cup when I drank from it, meaning…"

Slowly, too slowly for his tastes, the light bulbs went on over his subordinates' heads. Ackers's eyes widened, his mouth forming a small "o," while Haverman looked sheepish.

"Somebody wanted Juniper dead," Haverman said.

Desmond felt his shoulders slump with relief

at them finally getting it. "Exactly," he said. "What I've been trying to figure out is who would want to get rid of her."

"It had to be somebody at the party," Ackers said. "Nobody else would have had access to the food and drinks."

"Obviously."

"We need to find out who all was there that night and see if any of them had a grudge."

Desmond nodded. He'd already made plans to pay a visit to Juniper in the morning. Normally, he would have already done so, but given that he'd been interrogating other suspects, and now the state of his head, he hadn't had either the time or the inclination to challenge her.

"I'll handle that bit," he said to both of them. "What I want you two to do is find out if she had caterers on site, and if so, find them and bring them in for questioning."

He began to gather his things. "For tonight, however, I suggest getting some sleep. I've got a feeling the next few days are going to be rather eventful."

CHAPTER TEN

*J*uniper grumbled all the way downstairs. Jacobi had wakened her moments before Anna knocked on her door to let her know she had a visitor. By the time she reached the bottom step and recognized who was waiting for her, she was too awake to march right back upstairs and fall asleep again easily—which she normally would have done upon discovering the man's identity—and still too sleepy to be a genial hostess.

"Oh, good grief, McQuackers. What are you doing here at the buttcrack of dawn? Go home. Go back to bed. You can come back at ten, or how about never? I have a Christmas gathering to plan and a murder to solve, and I don't need any of this," she said, waving her finger back and forth to indicate the air between the two of them.

"I know the coffee was meant for you, Juniper. Uh, Ms. Holiday, I mean. The cup I drank from—I wasn't the target. It was you—and that's just what I've been explaining to your butler."

Juniper frowned. "Terrence is the one who let you in at this ungodly hour of the morning?"

"What? No, I—" Desmond paused then shook his head. "No, Ms. Holiday. I thought I mentioned it was your butler to whom I was speaking."

"You did." Juniper nodded. "My butler's name is Terrence, or have you forgotten already?"

Desmond's frown was almost comical as he considered her words. "Maybe. I—I could have sworn he introduced himself as Lionel."

"Lionel?" Juniper's brows almost touched her hairline. "You saw Lionel, McDuckman? Are you certain?"

"He is most certain, Ms. Holiday. I am

THANKSGIVING DINNER DEATH

pleased to have made the detective's rather enlightened acquaintance just this morning." Lionel floated into the room through the door to verify the detective's statement. "I will admit I stayed precisely at floor level, mum. I thought it best to do so—at least until you arrived."

Desmond blinked once. Twice. Then he grabbed his temples between the fingers and thumb of his right hand. "I'm sorry, Ms. Holiday, I thought—I believe—I—maybe I, too, am more sleep deprived than I thought."

Instead of showing concern, Juniper howled with laughter. "You can see Lionel! Oh my stars! Now there's a twist I'll admit I never saw coming!"

She raced to the door and called for others to join them, only one of whom he knew. "Tori! Felicity! Jacobi, come quick! There's something in the library you simply have to see!"

Tori was first to arrive. "Juniper, you scared me half to death with your yelling! What in the world is going on in here so early? The sun's barely up and…" Realizing they weren't alone, she said, "Oh. I'm sorry, Detective Mallard. What brings you here so early this morning?"

Juniper waved away her pretty speech. "Never mind that, Tor. There's something else you've gotta see—or not, as the matter may warrant."

The others joined the three already in the room, Desmond noticed. One rose through the very boards of the floor, and another descended through the ceiling. He paled, and Juniper's laugh turned into an unstoppable cackle.

"Jacobi, may I introduce to you Detective Desmond Mallard. Felicity, if you please, curtsey to the gentleman. Duckman, this is my cook and my housekeeper—the dead ones, that is. Lionel here is my previously deceased butler."

Though his gaze never wavered, and he nodded at all the appropriate times, she could tell he was having a very hard time with believing what his own eyes were showing him.

"You've already met Sabrina, Terrence, and Anna, at the Halloween bash, I believe. Those three members of my staff are, of course, still alive. But I'm thrilled to finally have someone with the sight to be able to see the others."

Rather than inquire of Juniper directly, the detective turned his sights on Tori. "Is she saying these people are ghosts?"

Tori glanced around, her expression one of confusion. "Desmond, I have to tell you there's no one else in the room besides yourself, June, and me, but if she's introducing the people she 'talks to' sometimes, yes. Juniper swears the place is haunted… No, wait. She says we have ghosts living here among us."

He closed his eyes and opened them again, his expression suddenly filled with hope—perhaps that he would no longer see them. "They are still here, Tori, as plain as you and me. They came in through the door, floor, and ceiling, but…" His hand went up to cover his face, and he rubbed at his eyes. "I think it must be a delayed reaction to the poison, because I am most definitely hallucinating."

"Nope, not hallucinating, you old Duckster. Just seeing the world more clearly now that you've taken a stroll on the other side," Juniper told him as she grabbed his hand and pulled him toward a chair. "So… sit here. Take a load off, man, and tell me what you're doing here before I have my real-life staff throw you out again."

"Right." He nodded but there was confusion in his eyes. "The reason I am here. Yes."

Beside him, Tori sported a frown of concern. "June, do you think we should call for an ambulance again? He doesn't sound like himself or look so well."

"At a thousand bucks a trip, one way? Come on, Torster. You've got to be kidding." Waving away her worry, Juniper said, "He will be fine. Just give him a bit for the truth to sink in."

"That he's seeing ghosts?" Tori asked.

Juniper nodded. "Of course. What did you think I meant?"

"The poison. It was meant for you," Desmond finally said. He turned his gaze upon Juniper and said, "Someone tried to kill you at your Thanksgiving dinner party, Juniper Holiday. And now, somehow, I have to find a way to protect you."

"Protect? Moi? You?" Juniper laughed. "Wow, did you hear that, Tori? The Duckman came here to offer his addled protection!"

"Juniper, I think you should mind your manners just now," Tori scolded. "Can't you see he's trying his best to offer his help despite all the crap you give him? The horrible names, the disdainful tone of your voice when you speak to him, the…"

Juniper held up her hand. "Oh, save it, Tori. I know why he came, but we already figured it out last night. Someone tried to kill me at my own party, and you want to help me figure out who it is."

CHAPTER ELEVEN

*D*esmond couldn't believe the nerve of Juniper acting as if *she* would find the killer and *he* would need her help! But he actually did need her help with one thing: the guest list.

She'd been nice enough to comply, so later that afternoon, he sat in her study, going over the list. He couldn't remember the last time he'd had this much trouble concentrating on a task. Then again, he'd never had to deal with an apparition floating at his elbow, either. He cleared his throat and looked up at… Lionel, was it? Or was it Jacobi? He couldn't be sure. He knew they were male, though.

"Could you back up a couple of paces? I

can't focus with you standing so close. I feel like I'm going to literally bump into you, and I don't think that would be very pleasant for either of us."

The ghost looked at him for a moment, as if he was assessing him, then gave a nod and floated back a few inches.

"Thank you."

Desmond returned his attention to the list. A ghostly hand floated into view, its ethereal form providing a bluish-gray haze over the paper as it pointed at a name. "I don't suppose you've brought that one in for questioning already?"

Desmond frowned, wondering at the soundness of the ghost's mind, which was a strange thing to be thinking about, all things considered. "No," he said. "Philippa Collins isn't a person of interest at the moment."

Mainly because she had a foot in the grave already and was more than a little senile. The sweet woman was off in her own world inside her head when she was awake and had an army of nurses looking after her. It couldn't have been her.

The ghost sniffed. "All right. You're the detective. You obviously know what's best."

Desmond couldn't help but feel the ghost was being condescending.

"Jackie boy, Philippa couldn't hurt a fly, much less poison me," Juniper said as she breezed into the room. "Besides, she loves me. Always has." To Desmond, she said, "You 'bout got that list narrowed down, Quackers?"

No. No, he did not. But he wasn't about to tell Juniper that. Looking at the paper, then at her, he said, "Yes."

"Good," she said with a sharp nod. "Because I'm tired of you being in my house. Why don't you pack it up and go home forever?"

"Juni—Ms. Holiday," he corrected, "I would love nothing more than to do that very thing, but you did agree to go over this list with me, and yet you've made yourself scarce the entire time I've been here. Surely you, better than anyone, know who might have it out for you."

Juniper put her hand on the desk he was using, resting her weight on it as she cocked her hip. "And I already told you you were wasting your time. Surely none of my guests would want to kill me. Well, with the exception of you."

Desmond groaned, which was very unlike

him, and pinched the bridge of his nose between his thumb and forefinger. "Why would I poison your coffee and then drink it myself?"

"Why do you do a good many things you do, Desmond? How do I know you haven't spent years building up an immunity to poison, hmm?"

Desmond gave her a flat stare. "Does me dying not answer that question for you?"

"You could've faked it."

"I had no pulse, or so I've been told. You checked yourself."

Juniper pursed her lips. "Touché."

Desmond leaned back in his chair, crossing his arms over his chest. His eyes narrowed. "What about your friend Garrett? He could have done it. I seem to recall him being in my room right after I was revived."

Juniper snorted. "Gare Bear loves me. He wouldn't hurt me, much less try to kill me. And if you really believed he was responsible for the poison, why haven't you brought him in?"

"You wanna do my job, Ms. Holiday?"

"No," Juniper said on an airy sigh. "Too boring, too tedious, and too restrictive for me, D-Man. I prefer to live life hard and fast. Otherwise, you end up a shriveled old prune by the time you're forty, and God knows I wouldn't look good with those kinds of wrinkles."

He laughed despite himself. "I didn't try to kill you, Juniper. But if I had, you wouldn't be here right now."

Juniper's eyebrows slowly rose. "Ditto, detective. Poison's not really my style," she said with a wink then moved away from the desk. "Lunch is in ten if you want to stick around that long. Tori usually comes down to eat if she's not neck-deep in plot tangles. Please don't flirt with her in front of me, though. The last thing I need is an upset stomach."

Desmond rolled his eyes. "Flirting is the last thing on my mind at the moment, Ms. Holiday. If you haven't noticed, I'm trying to find out who tried to murder you."

"Well, you're taking your sweet time about it."

"What are you two arguing about now?" Tori asked as she joined her godmother and Desmond.

"I'm trying to convince your godmother to let me do my job, Ms. Cooper," Desmond said, looking pointedly at Juniper.

Tori's brows rose. "Good luck with that. I had a heck of a time convincing her to let me do my own homework growing up. Once she gets it in her head that she knows the right way to do something, then everything else is wrong, and you'd best get out of her way."

"I'm still in the room," Juniper said.

"Listen, I came down because I've stumbled across something in my research. The poison might not have been put in Juniper's drink by someone at the party," Tori said.

Juniper and Desmond frowned at Tori. "What? How could that be?"

"I was doing research for a book, and I came across something called a poison ring. It's a ring with a hidden compartment for poison. You simply hover your finger over a drink and open the compartment. The poison would then fall into the drink."

Juniper's eyes widened. "The ring that strange woman gave me!"

Desmond's frown deepened. "What ring?"

"You don't remember? I was wearing this ring some strange woman gave me. It fell into my coffee, and you fished it out. That's why you drank the coffee. Then you went facedown in the pie," Juniper said.

Desmond shook his head, confused. "No, I don't remember that at all. My memory is fuzzy. I guess that happens when you die."

"Do you think that woman meant to poison me?" Juniper asked. "But it doesn't make sense. She couldn't have known that the ring would fall into my drink. And besides, she said the ring would protect me."

Desmond held a hand up. "Hold on. Who is this woman, and where is this ring?"

Juniper told him about meeting Halen and how she'd given her the ring. "But don't you have the ring down at the station in evidence?"

"No, I don't remember seeing any ring at the station. Just the coffee cup." Desmond rubbed his temples. "This is all so confusing."

Juniper was quiet for a moment before she spoke again. "I think we need to find that woman and ask her some questions."

"Not to mention find the ring," Tori said. "It was right beside the coffee cup."

"Ackers and Haverman didn't mention any ring. Do you think someone could have taken it in the confusion?" Desmond asked.

Juniper pressed her lips together. "If they did, we need to find out who that was."

"We aren't sure there was poison in the ring, but it's something to look into," Tori pointed out. "I'm pretty sure lunch is ready, so let's go eat, shall we? I declare food time truce time, so I don't wanna hear either of you arguing at the table. Got it?"

"I will be on my best behavior, Ms. Cooper," Desmond replied.

Juniper snorted loudly. "All right, Casanova, pack the papers away, and let's get food in you. We'll crack down on the list and find out more about the ring afterward."

As Desmond followed Juniper and Tori into the kitchen, where they took their meals when Juniper wasn't entertaining, he felt an odd sense of belonging. He wasn't sure how to feel about it, but for now, he would simply let it be. Chances were he'd go right back to wanting to strangle Juniper whenever their paths crossed, but for now, he could pretend that he was part of whatever it was that made up this strange little family that lived in a mansion at the tip of the cove.

CHAPTER TWELVE

While Anna cleared lunch from the table, Tori and Juniper followed Desmond back into the front parlor. "I really hope the person who tried to kill my godmother doesn't make another attempt."

"Hmm... I think Juniper can take care of herself. I mean, she managed to dodge the last attempt pretty easily."

"Ha! Unlucky for you, though. But I still don't think it was one of my guests. I hope you're looking into the people we hired as well," Juniper said. "And now we have the strange ring lady to investigate too."

Desmond frowned and pointed at the guest list. "Are you saying you won't even try to connect any of the names on this list with what happened? Surely there are any number of people who came to your dinner who don't actually like you, Ms. Holiday. Those people might have a motive, unlike some stranger who gave you a ring."

Juniper did a double take and actually looked affronted.

"Excuse me? I'll bet there are more on there that don't like *you*, Mr. Waddlebutt. But—" She held up her hand. "In the interest of fairness, I will tell you what Tori thinks. Well, maybe not what she really thinks, but it's at least what she said."

When she fell silent, her look expectant, Desmond threw out both his hands. "Well? Please, enlighten me, Ms. Holiday. What did your goddaughter say?"

Juniper laughed at his obvious exasperation then waved a hand to dismiss it all. "Oh, the enlightenment part already happened. You're gonna have to get used to living with ghosts now."

His expression closed. "The other part. Your goddaughter. What did she have to say?"

"Oh, that." Juniper flopped down onto the

sofa and picked up a magazine. "She said it was probably Beatrice Miller who tried to kill me. Said the woman hates all the noise and to-do up here at the mansion. And that's something you should know already, too, since she calls the cops on us almost every night."

Desmond's brow lowered. "And was she a guest at your dinner?"

"Sure she was. She's practically our next-door neighbor, Desi-D. We couldn't exactly ignore her, now, could we? Especially after all the time and effort she puts into harassing us." Juniper snorted. "The woman is harmless, Dez. Just a sad, pruny old giver-upper. Her life ended a long time ago, and she's too bitter to try and do anything to change it—so she gets her thrills by bugging Tori and me over the music and the events I hold here."

"I see." Desmond put a mark beside the woman's name anyway, and Juniper snorted again. "Gonna check her out because Toribell said it, are ya? I get it. I see where your loyalties lie now."

"I'm going to speak with her, yes, but mostly because you want to overlook her," Desmond said while pointing at her with the rolled-up guest list papers. "In the meantime, you can forget any amateur investigating ideas you have."

Juniper crossed her arms over her chest. "I'm no amateur, Quackers. I'm gonna go upstairs to my office and work on my Christmas wingding. Make a list, check it twice. You gonna be on there? Depends. Are you naughty or nice?"

"I'm sure you will decide regardless of what I think."

Juniper laughed. "There ya go. Get with the program, DeeDee. You're too straitlaced and uptight to be naughty, and that's bad. Too much the do-gooder type to be really nice—more condescending. Blech. I like my men to be men, ya know? And so does Tori, judging from the men she creates in those books she writes. Oh, wait. I forgot which planet you came from. You probably don't read, either, so never mind."

"Is that all, Ms. Holiday?" Desmond's shoulders and spine were now stiff, to say nothing of his expression.

"Yes, as a matter of fact, it is," Juniper said, her head bobbing in a repetitive nod. "Don't let the door bump you in the bootay on your way out unless you wanna hit your head on my marble floor."

Tori, who had been silent since Juniper had walked into the room, cast him an apologetic look. "I'll walk you out, Detective Mallard."

"Truce over when the crumbs are gone, I see," he told her as they walked through the foyer to the front door. Tori nodded.

"Absolutely, but it works for me. And June. She has to play nice while we're eating, and I let her do her thing almost all the rest of the time. It's a win-win situation, at least in this house." She stopped. "Thanks for checking in with us today, Desmond. Do give us a call if you find anything."

After Mallard left, Juniper hurried to her car. He'd asked her a few questions about where he might find Halen, and even though it seemed as if he was focusing on her party guest list, she knew that he'd be seeking out the mysterious ring-giving woman, and Juniper wanted to make sure she got to her first.

CHAPTER THIRTEEN

*J*uniper pulled up near the WitchRoast Café, waiting for the last bit of Led Zeppelin's "Immigrant Song" to end before she killed the engine and got out. A cool gust of wind slipped past the edges of her coat, making her shiver, and she tucked her hands into the pockets as she stepped up onto the sidewalk.

The cafe was tucked between the Dusty Buns Bakery and the flower shop. The only thing that was missing on this little stretch of street was a bookstore to complete the cozy aesthetic. They'd make a killing during the fall and winter months, that was for sure. People liked somewhere warm and cozy to read after they'd picked up something warm to eat. Buy a book, get some rolls, spend a few hours at the coffee shop eating your spoils while getting lost in whatever words you'd chosen that day. It would be perfect.

Leaves crunched beneath her boots as she walked to her destination, and that wonderful fall smell teased her nose before she stepped inside the cafe and was greeted with the aromas of warm pastries and glorious coffee.

Quincy nodded to her when he saw her as he finished taking a customer's order then held up a finger, indicating he'd get hers going in just a second.

Juniper went to her usual table near the windows and waited for Quincy to finish up with the few other people in the cafe before getting to her. As she waited, she rubbed the naked spot on her pinky finger and glanced around, looking for Halen.

"Here ya go. One extra-large, extra-strong black coffee."

Juniper looked up as Quincy slid into the empty chair across from her. "Do you know why someone would want me dead, Quince?"

Quincy, bless him, didn't bat an eyelash at

her question. "June, honey, why anyone would want to rid the world of your zest for life is beyond me."

A smile tugged at the corners of her mouth. "You know the poison you cured the Duck Man of was meant for me, don't you?"

It was Quincy's turn to frown. "I didn't. I'm sorry, June. Any clue who might have done it?"

She shook her head. "Been trying to figure it out, though. Not a lot to go on. There's not exactly a string of clues lying around. We just know there was poison—pretty potent poison to have offed the detective as fast as it did too. So somebody around here has to have solid knowledge of poisons."

"It wasn't me, Juniper," Quincy said, holding her gaze. "And the coven here is more interested in healing people than hurting them. If they intended harm, I would know."

"You know them that well, do you?"

"The oath they swore was a spell, binding their very souls unto death. If they break it, their ability to do magic is stripped from them, and all knowledge of us or our abilities is wiped from their memories. Essentially, they end up forever trying to remember something important only to never know what it was. Their names are also stricken from the coven's records, and they are banished."

Juniper's eyes widened a little more with each thing he listed. "Wow. Yeah, okay, you know them pretty well."

Quincy nodded then motioned to her hand, where she was still fiddling with her finger. "Where's your ring?"

"I'd like to know that as well," Juniper said. "I haven't seen it since the night of the poisoning. I was wearing it then. It fell into my cup of coffee, which the detective ingested and died from. I was wondering if the poison could have been in the ring."

Quincy was already shaking his head before Juniper had even finished speaking. "Halen wouldn't do that. She might be on the New Age side of things, but she just wants to help people. If she gave you the ring, it was for a reason. Why you can't find it now, I don't know. Besides, that ring was a protection ring, and anyway, how could enough poison to kill someone be in a small ring?"

He had a point.

"How do you know the ring was a protection ring?"

"I saw the stone. Black tourmaline. It's for protection. And I might be reaching here, but if it fell into your coffee before Detective Mallard drank it, it probably mitigated some of the poison."

"The man was deader than a doornail, Quince. You saw him."

"I did," he said, smiling at her wording. "But it could have been worse. And anyway, the ring did protect *you*, apparently, since it caused you to not drink the poison."

He had made some good points. Juniper took a drink of her coffee, sighing appreciatively at the taste as she made a mental note to find out what type of poison Desmond had ingested and how much of it one would need to kill someone.

"Hang in there, Juni girl. Somebody will figure out who tried to get rid of you. I just hope it's either you or the detective who finds out first because if it was one of us, there's no guarantee justice won't be taken out of their hide, if you know what I mean."

Juniper's chest filled with warmth at the thought of her friends caring about her so deeply. Smiling at Quincy, she leaned forward and patted his hand. "I appreciate the devotion, Quince, but please don't hurt someone on my account."

"We won't hurt 'em too bad, June. Just enough that they learn their lesson." Quincy nodded toward the big window that overlooked Main Street. "If you want to catch Halen, there she is right out there."

Juniper whirled around just in time to catch a glimpse of the dark-haired girl sauntering past the window.

"Gotta go!" She jumped up, threw some money onto the table, and ran for the door.

By the time Juniper got outside, Halen was half a block away, and she was walking fast.

"Hey, Halen! Wait up!"

Juniper expected her to run. That was no problem; she was pretty good at chasing people down. But Halen didn't run. Instead, she turned and waited for Juniper to jog over to her.

"I hear the ring worked." Halen directed her gaze at Juniper's hand, her eyes registering surprise upon noticing her fingers were bare. "But where is it?"

Juniper looked down, half expecting the ring to appear. It didn't. "Never mind that. The ring wasn't for protection. It poisoned someone!"

Halen crossed her arms over her chest. "I don't know what you mean. You're unharmed."

"I am, but Detective Mallard wasn't. Tell me the truth: What was in the ring?"

"I told you before. It's a protection stone."

"Then why was full of poison?"

"Why do you keep saying that? It was a black tourmaline," Halen said as if that settled it.

"Well, I don't care what kind of stone it was. That ring fell into my coffee and almost killed the Detective. Well, actually, it did kill him, but he came back."

Halen looked confused.

"Never mind. My point is that the ring had something on it or in it that made my coffee lethal."

"If it was your coffee that was lethal, then how did the detective get harmed?"

"The ring fell into my coffee, and he fished it out. Then, when I said I wouldn't drink it because he'd had his fingers in it, he drank it." Juniper realized how silly that sounded.

"Aha! See, the ring did protect you. It fell into the cup to keep you from drinking that coffee." She pressed her lips together. "Maybe I need to give Detective Mallard a ring too."

Juniper wasn't about to just believe Halen. Naturally, the woman wouldn't admit to poisoning her. But if she had done it, then why was she standing here as innocent as could be? "I don't know whether I believe you. That ring could have been a poison ring, and maybe it was just good luck on my part that Mallard was the one to drink the poison."

"What's a poison ring?"

Juniper studied the other woman and concluded that she seemed to really not know what a poison ring was. "It's a ring with a little compartment that you can put something in, like poison, and then covertly open it up over a drink. Your victim will never know who did it."

"That's just silly. How would I know the ring was going to open at the right time?"

She had a point.

"I've already told you, the ring was for protection. It didn't have any compartment." Her gaze flicked to Juniper's hand again. "But I'd say if you've lost that ring, then you should find it, because without it, you might be unprotected. You still know a lot of secrets about Crescent Cove, and maybe some people want to make sure those secrets don't get out."

CHAPTER FOURTEEN

*B*ack at home, Tori was putting the finishing touches on a chapter when she heard a noise downstairs. "Terrence? Anna? That you? I'm in here. June's not back from coffee, but I'm sure we'll hear her screaming in soon."

Barclay raised his head from his nap and growled.

No one answered. Usually, Tori would shrug it off and go back to her work, but the attempt on her godmother's life, combined with Barclay's reaction, was far too recent for her to ignore bumps like that. Picking up the baseball bat Juniper had bought her at the first baseball game they'd seen together when she was only nine years old, Tori left the room and crept down the stairs. At the bottom, she turned around and almost ran smack into Garrett.

"Oh my word! Garrett! Who let you in? What are you doing here?"

Barclay stopped growling and wagged his tail as Garrett bent to pet him. Luna, Loki, and Finn, on the other hand, hissed at the poor man and ran off.

"Is that any way to treat a close, trusted friend?" he asked, a tinge of pretend hurt in his tone as he looked up at her. Then he laughed. "I'm here to see Juni, actually. Quincy said she'd been by the café, and I figured I'd catch her here sooner or later. Terry let me in, then he disappeared into the mansion. I guess he meant for me to make myself at home."

Before she could comment, the sound of Phil Collins's "In the Air Tonight" thumped against the windows, rattling them in their frames. Tori cast a look at Garrett. "Speak of the devil and she shall appear."

He chuckled then sweetly reprimanded her. "Aw, now, June's not that bad. In fact, she's rather fun if you ask me—unlike most of the current occupants living in the Cove. At least she's not afraid to do what she wants the way she wants to do it. She's a free spirit, and we would be breaking some natural law somewhere if we tried to tame her."

"Absolutely." Tori nodded. "She's a one hundred percent mess if you ask me, but I'd never ask her to change a thing. She keeps me on my toes and motivated to push harder, do more, and keep those limits where they're supposed to be: removed."

"No. Nope, someone tried, but it didn't work," Juni said as she pushed the front door open with her hip, since her hands were full with packages she had hauled inside. "Besides, I'm harder to remove than you give me credit for, dear."

Garrett laughed. "We were just saying how we would never even try, June. We love you too much for that."

"Good thing too." She kicked the door shut and hurried into the parlor to put her packages down. "Don't either of you rush to help, ya hear? You might hurt yourselves in the excitement."

Tori rolled her eyes, pointed at Juniper, and whispered, "See? A total mess."

Juniper ignored her. "Glad to see you're not in jail, Garrett. Your wife said the Duckpin brought you in."

Garrett laughed. "They just had a few questions."

"And did you learn anything from them?"

"Not a thing. Between you and me, I don't think they have a clue."

"I was afraid of that." Juniper opened one of the boxes and pulled out a silver tinsel garland. "What do you think about this for the stairway?"

"You're certainly wasting no time making the transition from Thanksgiving to Christmas, but I suspect that's not the only place you've been this afternoon," Tori said.

"Ahhh, the suspicious mind of a mystery author. You're right. I was doing some investigating of my own since, as Garrett has verified, I doubt the police have a clue." Juniper told them about her visit to WitchRoast and her conversation with Halen.

"But this Halen person could be lying," Tori pointed out.

"Of course, but I kind of got the vibe she

wasn't," Juniper said. "And she wasn't here at the dinner, so what happened to the ring?"

Garrett frowned. "Wait a minute. You said that it fell into your coffee, and the detective fished it out and put it on the napkin next to the cup, right?"

"Yep. Then he drank the coffee, and you know what happened next."

"You might want to check with Fedora Layhee," Garrett said. "You know how she loves her beads and baubles, and as we were hauling Mallard out, I noticed her lurking around where you had been sitting. I thought she was just after the pie, but…"

Garrett let his voice trail off, and Juniper glanced in the direction of Fedora's house. "But Fedora wouldn't try to poison me."

"No, but she might have seen something or know something. And that ring is evidence, so if she has it, it might be smart to get it back," Tori said.

"That's good thinking." Juniper opened a few more boxes then propped her hands on her hips. "I'm stuck for a Santa, Garrett. You wanna dress up in the red suit and hand out gifts on Christmas Eve?"

His eyes went wide. "Good wolf, no. Not me, Juniper Holiday, and don't even bother setting out to be conniving. I have to be at Rarely Done most of the day, anyway, so playing Santa really would not fit in my schedule."

"Poop," Juniper pouted. "I guess that means I'll have to run an ad and hire someone... unless one of you has a suggestion."

"You could always ask Desmond," Tori teased, enjoying the spark of fire that suddenly lit Juniper's eyes.

"Girl, I should disown you for that. But I won't, because I'll never get all the Christmas decorations up by myself," she threatened.

Garrett laughed. "I'll help with those if I get a chance, but count me out for Santa."

"Yeah, 'cause you're too big a turkey to play Father Christmas is all," Juniper grumped yet again. Then she smiled. "I'm really glad you brought Lyra for Thanksgiving, Gar. And I'm really sorry our mystery poisoner almost ruined it for everyone—especially for the Duck Man. Yeesh."

"We're just glad you're safe and everything turned out well for the detective, June." He turned to leave. "I'm gonna head out now. Just wanted to check in to see if you'd discovered anything about the poisoning."

Knock, knock, knock.

Juniper looked at Tori, who in turn looked at Garrett, a question in her eyes. "Who could that be?"

A few seconds later, Terry ushered in Harvey Nichols from the police department.

"Ms. Holiday, Ms. Cooper." Harvey nodded at them then frowned at Garrett. "I'm afraid we got another complaint from your neighbor about a noise violation."

Tori's head dropped back, and she groaned. "Beatrice again. I swear, that woman must have the most sensitive set of ears on the planet."

"Wouldn't top mine," Garrett joked.

"We'll keep it down, officer." Tori ushered the man back out and then returned.

"The nerve of her!" Juniper said. "After I invited her to Thanksgiving dinner. I'm going to give her a piece of my mind."

Juniper started for the door, but Tori grabbed her elbow. "I don't think that's such a good idea. Didn't you ever hear that you catch more flies with honey than with vinegar?"

"Honey schmoney. That woman needs a talking-to."

"I'll go," Tori said. "Don't forget that Beatrice is one of the suspects in your attempted murder, and this could be our one chance to size her up for clues. Probably wouldn't be good for you to march over there all mad. It will take a clear head to find out what she knows about the poisoning and maybe even get her to confess."

CHAPTER FIFTEEN

While Tori went to Beatrice's house, Juniper headed to Fedora's. Unfortunately, the woman wasn't home. That was okay, though. Juniper needed to collect another piece of information, and it could only be obtained from the police or the hospital. She figured her chances were much better at the hospital.

Before she was out of Fedora's driveway, she'd already hit the play button on one of her favorite Mötley Crüe CDs. Within seconds, "Shout at the Devil" blared from the convertible, alerting everyone in the vicinity that Juniper Holiday was on the road again. As she passed Beatrice's house, she couldn't resist a smile. "Take that, you old witch."

But as the house sped by in her rearview mirror, Juniper's smile became a frown. What in the world happened to a body, she wondered, to make them turn out as crotchety and bitter as Beatrice had? There had been plenty of bad times, sad times, and things to make her go crazy in Juniper's life, but she'd refused to let any of them shut her down.

Forget about the attempt to poison Juniper; it was a wonder someone hadn't tried to kill Beatrice!

Head bobbing in time to the music as she sang along, Juniper rounded a bend, flipped on her turn signal, then hit the brakes. Her tires squealed as she made the turn. At the moment, she was in it to win it, and right now, simply driving was winning.

A few minutes later, she pulled into a parking space and looked up. The words Crescent Cove General Hospital stood in relief on the top third of the building. Reaching for her purse, Juniper got out of the car and headed inside. Five minutes later, she was schmoozing the doctor who had treated the Duckster the night he'd been poisoned and died right at her dinner table, his face planted in pie.

"So, the poison. Did you guys or the boys at the station run a toxicology test?" she asked.

Doctor Everly Mason nodded. "Yes, of course. The police will have that on file."

Juniper shook her head. "Such a shame, really. The poor detective must have been in shock. Who even does such things as poison someone these days, anyway, and where do they find the poison?"

The doctor spread his hands wide. "Wish I could tell you, June, but some people will be as evil as the day is long. Who knows what drives them?"

"Not much," Juniper mumbled in an aside. "Folk like that can't have much going on in the intelligence department, right?"

Again, he shrugged. "Not for me to say, but if you'd like, I could put in a call to one of the guys over at the precinct. See what they found out? I'd love to tell you myself, but I'm not allowed."

Juniper declined as sweetly as she could. If

McDuckster ever found out she'd been poking around for information in the case of his own death, he'd be livid.

"I think it'll all come out in the wash, anyway, Doc. Thanks for the chat and the coffee," she said, holding up her little Styrofoam cup, "but I think I'll see myself out."

Dr. Mason waved goodbye. "Till next time, Juni! You take care of yourself!"

"Always!" she assured him as she walked toward the exit, making sure to keep smiling until she was out of sight.

In the car, she placed the folder she'd snitched and shoved into her oversized tote on the seat beside her and quickly flipped through it. What she found had her snorting and shaking her head. Desmond Mallard was as fit as a fiddle and as strong as an ox. There was not one single ding in his medical report... except for the fact that he'd died and that he'd had traces of water hemlock in his system.

A Google search for water hemlock revealed that it was a weed-like plant resembling Queen Anne's lace and, more importantly, an amount small enough to fit inside a poison ring could be lethal.

She jammed the car into reverse and headed back toward Fedora's house. She needed to find that ring!

CHAPTER SIXTEEN

*B*eatrice Miller was the exact opposite of Juniper in every way a person could be. Where Juniper was loud and outspoken, Beatrice was quiet and reserved. She was the quintessential grandmotherly type, complete with short curly gray hair. She also didn't stand taller than five feet three inches. She looked sweet enough, but behind those soft cheeks and kind brown eyes lurked a harridan of the first degree.

Tori was convinced she disliked anything fun on principle, and she wouldn't know how to let loose and have a good time if somebody walked her through the steps. Quite frankly, Tori was tired of Beatrice trying to rain on their parade because she didn't like that Juniper was having fun.

Walking up to her front door, she reached for the gaudy cherub knocker and slammed it down a handful of times then stepped back and waited for someone to answer the summons.

Movement around the side of the house caught her eye. Beatrice's maid was picking herbs in the garden. Tori was surprised any were growing this late in the season, but there were still quite a few, though they looked a bit weedy.

She recognized basil, parsley, and... wait. Was that white lacy flower water hemlock? Tori knew it was poisonous from her book research. But she also knew a lot of other plants resembled it, like Queen Anne's lace and even carrots. She leaned closer and squinted for a better look.

Just then, the door opened, and Juniper jerked her attention back to see Beatrice standing there.

"Hello," she said in a syrupy-sweet voice. "How can I help you?"

Tori forced a smile. It wouldn't do to bite the old woman's head off. "Hi, Mrs. Miller. I thought I'd stop by for a little chat if you don't mind."

"Oh, but it's past two, dear."

"Which is the perfect time for tea, don't you think?" Tori suggested, doing her best not to snarl.

Beatrice looked at her as if she'd just done the worst thing possible to disappoint her. "Tea isn't until four, dear. But I suppose I'll make an exception for you this once."

With a worried glance back at the garden—that *was* just Queen Anne's lace, wasn't it?—Tori thanked her and followed her inside, where the differences between Beatrice and her godmother became all the more apparent. While the Holiday mansion was open and spacious, mirroring Juniper's take on life, Beatrice's home was packed to the gills with sundry knickknacks and baubles. There wasn't an inch of space free on the wallpapered walls; every bit of them was covered in shelving or pictures. The floors were decorated with heavy, gaudy carpets that clashed with the rest of the room. The place was spick and span and smelled of spiced gingerbread, which put Tori in mind of the witch in "Hansel and Gretel." Luckily, Beatrice didn't seem the type to gobble up little kids, let alone a full-grown woman.

Beatrice led her to a little receiving room decorated in pinks and golds, with matching furniture. Beatrice took the love seat and directed Tori to sit in the high-backed chair across from her. Then she picked up a little bell from the coffee table and gave it a hearty ring.

A moment later, a tall, thin girl came into the room. Tori recognized her as one of the extra servers from their Thanksgiving dinner. She was probably trying to save up enough money to get out of Beatrice's employ. How she got by working for someone like Beatrice was a mystery.

"Tea, Poppy," Beatrice said sharply. "And some of that banana bread I made earlier this morning."

Poppy dipped a curtsey. "Yes, ma'am."

The second Poppy was gone, Beatrice smiled at Tori. "One has to be strict with the young ones these days. They think they know it all and don't have to answer for anything. If they work for me, I make sure they earn every penny they take home."

"I'm sure you do," Tori said.

"Oh, now, don't look so sour. My staff will be well provided for when I'm gone… as long as they do the work while I'm here."

"Mrs. Miller, I don't want to take up too much of your time today, so I'll get straight to the point. Do you have a vendetta against my godmother or something?"

Beatrice lurched back as though Tori had struck her. "Heavens no, child," she denied, pressing a hand to her neck as though to protect it. "Why would you think that?"

"Maybe the fact that you call the cops on us on the regular?" Tori said, brow arched.

Beatrice shook her head. "There's so much screeching going on over there at all hours, I just want to make sure everyone is all right, dearie."

"So you call the cops about noise violations instead of coming over yourself to check up on your neighbors?"

Beatrice gave her a sugary smile. "Sweetie, at my age, one cannot be expected to be running about all the time. It's… indecent."

Tori gave her a look. "Beatrice, you're barely older than Juniper. She's as spry as any twentysomething I know."

Beatrice gave a sigh. "That godmother of

yours tries too hard to fit in with the young folk, I fear. She should act her age. Maybe then she would find a fellow willing to settle down with her."

Poppy came in with the tea, preventing Tori from saying something nasty. This woman was clearly living in the far-distant past. She felt sorry for Beatrice.

Beatrice picked up the sugar tongs, and Tori took the opportunity to see if she was wearing Juniper's ring. She wasn't, but that didn't mean that she didn't have it stashed away somewhere. But why would she take it?

Tori managed to be polite as they sipped the tea and ate the banana bread. Truth be told, she couldn't wait to get out of there. Finally, she patted her lips with the napkin. "Well, this has been lovely."

"It has," Beatrice said.

"One more thing before I go," Tori said, standing. "Could you maybe call us and ask us to turn down the music next time? I'm sure the police will appreciate it."

Beatrice laughed. "Oh, I think they like doing their job plenty well, child. I wouldn't want them to think they weren't appreciated."

"Mm-hmm." Tori nodded and made her way from the room. "I can find my way out. Thanks for the tea. Goodbye now."

She opened the door and almost crashed into Poppy, who had been hovering just outside the door. She took the girl by the shoulders and promised she could have a better place of employment if she wanted to work for Juniper instead, which almost moved the girl to break down in tears.

CHAPTER SEVENTEEN

"Why, Juniper! How nice to see you." Fedora shoved her hands into the pockets of her loose-fitting smock and nudged the door shut with her foot.

"Fedora Layhee, are you hiding something?"

"Whyever would you say that?" Fedora wasn't a very good liar.

"Let's see your hands." Juniper gestured to the pockets.

Fedora laughed. "That's silly. You've seen my hands before."

"Listen. Somebody tried to poison my coffee at my own Thanksgiving dinner, and you were seen hovering around the scene of the crime, and something is missing: the ring that fell into my coffee. Do you happen to know anything about it? I would hate to have to have the police interrogate everyone that was seen near the table…"

Fedora's face turned crimson. "I didn't steal it. I mean, it was sitting right there on the table, and I didn't want it to get lost. I figured I'd keep it for you." Fedora took her hand out of the pocket and wiggled her fingers. The ring that Halen had given Juni was right there on her index finger.

Juniper held out her hand, and Fedora pried the ring off and plunked it into her palm.

"I was going to give it back."

Juniper turned the ring over, looking for a hinge or compartment, but there wasn't one. It was a normal ring with a big stone. "There's no compartment in this ring."

"Well, it's the one that was on the table." Fedora sounded a little defensive.

"I wasn't questioning that." Juniper had a great memory, and she could see it was the same ring. "Tori thought it might've been a poison ring with the poison in the compartment. She thought that was how it might have gotten into my coffee."

Fedora gasped and rubbed her hand.

"But I guess it wasn't. So the question remains: How did the poison get into my cup?"

Fedora's brows shot up. "I hope you don't think I had anything to do with it. Why don't you look at that maid of Beatrice Miller's? Penny or Petra or whatever her name is. She was having a big argument with one of the other servers about your special cup. You know, the one with the pansies that you like to drink out of."

"What do you mean?" Juniper remembered seeing the maid but hadn't noticed any argument.

"When they were serving the coffee, remember you told the server to take your cup back because you wanted the pansy one?"

Juniper nodded.

"Well, it turns out Beatrice's maid was filling that cup. When the server went back to get it, there was a little bit of an argument." Fedora gasped. "Oh my! You don't think the maid put the poison in the coffee? But why would Beatrice's maid want to poison you?"

"That's a good question. I barely know her." Juniper pressed her lips together. Then her eyes widened. "Oh no! I think we've gotten it all wrong!"

CHAPTER EIGHTEEN

*J*uniper rushed back to the mansion, getting to the front door at just the same time as Tori.

"I think I know who the killer is!" they said in unison.

"Wait… who do you think it is?" Juniper asked.

"Beatrice." Tori sounded confident, but then she started to look a bit uncertain. "At least, I think so. She has some plants in her garden that I think could be water hemlock."

"Hemlock!" Juniper gasped. "Mallard's file from the hospital showed traces of water hemlock in his system."

Tori frowned. "How did you see Desmond's file? That's supposed to be confidential."

"Oh, umm…" Juniper snugged her tote closer to be sure Tori couldn't peek into it. "I have my ways. But I'm not sure it was Beatrice."

"Why not?"

"Fedora said that she saw Beatrice's maid fighting with another server over my coffee cup." Juniper took the ring out of her pocket. "By the way, Fedora did have the ring."

Tori took the ring and turned it over in her hand. "This isn't a poison ring."

"I know, so I was thinking maybe the poison wasn't in the ring. Maybe it was in the cup."

Tori's brows rose. "So maybe the ring did protect you?"

"Maybe." Juniper wasn't sure about that. Technically, she hadn't drunk the coffee because the ring had fallen into it and Mallard had fished it out. But that was just a big coincidence… wasn't it?

"So you think the poison was in the cup, and Beatrice's maid had something to do with it? Why would the maid want to poison you?" Tori asked.

"That's the thing. Maybe the poison wasn't

meant for me."

"Or maybe it was, and Beatrice was having her maid do her dirty work. She's not that nice to her hired help."

"Oh, I hadn't thought about that. Beatrice is just the type to have someone else do the deed." Juniper flopped down on the couch. "We need to figure out if that really is water hemlock in her garden. That would be evidence that she was involved."

"Good thinking," Tori agreed. "But how?" She moved to sit on the couch. Worrying her bottom lip between her teeth in thought, she said after a minute, "Should we call Desmond? Tell him what we've discovered?"

"Probably," Juniper replied. In reality, she hated to hand things over to the Duckman, but she also didn't want him to arrest her for withholding evidence. "But not until I've had a stiff drink. After the last few days I've had, I'd say I deserve it."

Juniper wasn't one to drink spirits regularly, choosing to save them for special occasions. But that didn't mean she didn't have a great appreciation for alcoholic beverages. They could be fun from time to time. And God knew she had amassed quite the collection of various liquors and wines from the great-aunt who'd left her the mansion and everything it held after her passing.

Going to the liquor cabinet set against the far wall, she poured herself a shot of Southern Comfort and tossed it back like a pro, then she chased it with another. Smacking her lips, she turned to Tori. "All right. Now you can call Ducky Dearest."

Twenty minutes later, the detective sat in the front parlor with them, looking around the room suspiciously.

"They're not waiting to surprise you, D-Man. They've got other things to do besides lurk in the woodwork," Juniper assured him.

Desmond cleared his throat. "Forgive me. I—"

"Don't worry about it," Juniper cut him off. She looked at Tori then back at Desmond. "Ahem. We called you here because we're pretty sure we know who tried to kill me."

"Pretty sure?" Desmond asked with a raised brow. "I need more than that, Ms. Holiday."

"Well, we have it narrowed down to a few suspects," Juniper said. "And I think I know how we can figure it out for sure."

"I hope you're not planning some harebrained scheme," Desmond said.

"It's not harebrained," Juniper said, smiling in that way that put Desmond instantly on guard. That smile meant trouble. "We've got a plan, detective. The question is, do you want in on it, or would you prefer to watch from the sidelines?"

Desmond didn't have to think twice before answering. "You know, I would love to be part of it, Ms. Holiday," he said in a way that meant the exact opposite, "but seeing that I am a man of the law, and you are you, I think it best I not know about any of it just yet. Just let me know when you plan on executing said plan, and I'll be sure to be nearby should things go awry."

"Okay, fine," Juniper said, shrugging. "No skin off my toes if you don't wanna have any fun. Just don't come crying to me when you realize how much you missed out on."

"Oh, don't worry, Ms. Holiday," Desmond began, getting up to leave. "I don't think that will be a problem."

CHAPTER NINETEEN

The coffee service was perfect. It had belonged to one of Juniper's ancestors several hundred years or so ago, she was sure. There was a sterling silver coffee urn and matching sugar and creamer. They used the same cups as they had for the Thanksgiving dinner, except Juniper's favorite with the pansies was missing, as it was still in police evidence. That was okay. If history was to repeat itself, as Juniper hoped, the actual cup wouldn't matter.

Places were set for Juniper, Tori, Garrett, and Beatrice. Poppy was busy in the kitchen, gathering scones and muffins that Sabrina had baked.

Tori had had no trouble persuading the

maid to come. Okay, she might have implied it was an interview of sorts, which had made it all the more attractive to the girl. Poppy knew Beatrice would be there, which was part of the plan. Luckily, Tori had discovered that Beatrice didn't mind her staff taking side jobs, and since this was Poppy's day off, it shouldn't be an issue.

Desmond, of course, had been invited. Only he would be late arriving. That was also part of the plan. Juni and Tori and Garrett had decided that if they created a distraction, the killer would take advantage of that to make her move.

The knocker sounded at precisely four—not a second earlier or later. Tori smirked at the woman's obsession with precision. "I'll get it. You all wait here."

A special table had been brought down from the attic—one the Duckman's crack team of investigators had wired. Every word from this moment forward was being streamed directly into the van hidden in the garage. Cameras had been tucked into the trim work as well. If someone tried their hand at poison again, there would be proof—one way or another.

"Beatrice! Hi!" Tori leaned in for a fake air kiss and a hug. "So glad you could make it!

Come on inside. Terrence will take your coat. Thank you, Terrence."

Once the "receiving" had been done, Tori led her toward the front parlor. "We've only been seated for a second ourselves," she told the woman. "Except for Detective Mallard. He tried, but the poor man just couldn't make it on time."

She tsked then motioned for Beatrice to sit between Juniper and Garrett. Her expression when she looked at him was hilarious. Still, she faked a smile and went around to squeeze in between the two.

"Perhaps the detective is still feeling a bit off after his ordeal at your Thanksgiving Day party, Juniper," she said. "At least, one would think it the cause—after all, punctuality should be part of an authoritative life."

So prim. So proper, Tori thought. If she were writing a book, this woman would no doubt end up being either the victim or the killer.

Poppy placed the tray of scones and muffins on the table.

Beatrice looked surprised to see her. "Oh, Poppy, I see you are making good use of your day off."

Poppy simply nodded and got busy pouring the coffee into the cups. Her back was to them, and Juniper couldn't quite see what she was doing.

A crash and clatter—something they had set up before—at the side entrance signaled Desmond's late arrival. Tori stood. "That must be Detective Mallard. I'll just go let him know where we are."

"I'll pick up whatever that was, Tori. Mallard must have knocked over the cart or something. Maybe the big pot that was sitting on it broke. I wouldn't want you to hurt yourself," Garrett said, getting up to follow her.

Juniper got up as well, but she only went to the door. From her position, she could see both the back door and the parlor—clearly enough to see firsthand what was happening with the coffee cups. She knew Beatrice's sense of politeness would prevail, and the woman wouldn't touch a drop until everyone was back in the room.

"Detective Mallard's here." Juniper moved back into the room. Tori, Garrett, and Desmond followed. The coffee had been poured, and Poppy had placed a steaming cup in front of everyone.

"It's so nice to have you here, Beatrice," Juniper said.

"Thank you." Beatrice glanced around the table. "Though I do find the choice of invitees a bit unusual."

"Oh, just good friends. I like to make sure everyone has enough caffeine."

Beatrice nodded and picked up her cup.

"But wait!" Juniper held her hand over Beatrice's cup. "I also like to make sure the staff has enough caffeine to keep them awake. Perhaps you'd like to give your cup to Poppy, and we can get you a fresh one."

Beatrice looked confused. "What? Well, that is highly unusual, but I guess you are a strange one."

Juniper held Beatrice's cup out toward Poppy, who resembled a deer caught in the headlights. "Poppy, why don't you join us?"

For one tense moment, everyone in the room watched Poppy with bated breath, wondering what her next move would be. People did crazy things when they were caught in bad situations, and no one actually wanted anyone else to get hurt.

Poppy stared at the cup, clearly uncomfortable. "No, thanks, ma'am. I'm just here to serve the coffee."

"No, really, go ahead. Drink up." Juniper got up and walked the cup over to her.

Poppy's eyes darted from the cup to Juniper to Detective Mallard. Then, suddenly, she pushed the cup away and made a run for the door. Juniper was ready and lunged after her.

A bit of a fracas ensued. Poppy tried to slow Juniper down by whipping the tablecloth from the table, causing the china to smash on the floor in front of Juniper. Coffee and scones went everywhere.

But it was to no avail because Desmond was waiting at the door, blocking Poppy's exit. He whipped out the handcuffs.

"Poppy Sanders, you're under arrest for the attempted murder of Beatrice Miller."

Beatrice glanced from Poppy to Desmond to Juniper. "My word, Juniper Holiday, you sure don't do anything the normal way. What in the world is this about?"

Juniper turned to Beatrice. "I'm afraid that poison that made Detective Mallard sick at the Thanksgiving dinner was meant for you."

"Me? But I don't understand."

"I guess Poppy didn't want to work for you anymore. She tried to poison you at the Thanksgiving dinner," Tori said. "Unfortunately, she didn't realize the cup she had intended to serve to you was Juniper's favorite. When one of the other servers insisted on bringing that cup to Juniper, Poppy could hardly refuse."

Beatrice's hand flew to her chest. "Oh dear."

"What I don't understand," Garrett said, "is why go to all the trouble to poison her here? She would have plenty of opportunities to kill Beatrice right in her home."

"I know why. If she did it at Beatrice's house, she would be one of only a few suspects, but there were dozens of people at the dinner. She was hoping to muddy the waters of the investigation with suspects. Maybe she was even planning on pinning it on me, since it's well known that I don't like Beatrice calling the cops on me for noise violations all the time." Juniper skewered Beatrice with her gaze.

"Oh dear, Juniper! I will never do that again. Why… I owe you my life!" Beatrice was teary-eyed.

Garrett cleared his throat. "I guess that makes sense. And then she tried again today, thinking she could blame you and say it was already in the cup. But why? If she didn't want to work for Beatrice, why not just quit?"

"I know why," Tori said. "Beatrice said she'd take care of her staff after she was gone. I assume there is something in her will."

Beatrice nodded. "That's right. Oh dear, this is just terrible. Poppy. Why?"

Poppy just stared at her. "Maybe you should be nicer to your staff, and they won't try to kill you."

Beatrice looked taken aback. "Maybe. Maybe I should. And to my neighbors too."

"Does that mean you won't call the cops on us anymore?" Juniper asked.

"I should say not! I will be forever in your debt."

Desmond finished reading Poppy her rights and took her away.

Beatrice got up to leave. "However can I thank you, Juniper?"

"No need to thank me. I'm just glad you're okay." Juniper sincerely meant it. She felt bad for Beatrice. Clearly, something had happened in her life to make her such a grump. Maybe she'd turn over a new leaf now.

"I'm sorry for calling the cops on you, Juniper. From now on, I'm going to be a good neighbor," Beatrice said as she left.

"Well, that was interesting," Garrett said. He waved his hand. "Sorry about the mess. Tor and I will clean it up for you."

"No, it's fine," Juniper said, waving her hand, dismissing the offer. "It's only porcelain. It's replaceable."

"Yes, but it will also cut you," Garrett said, already heading to the door for the broom. "I'll be back in a second. Tori, don't let her step on anything."

"As if that's going to happen," Juniper remarked flippantly and went to sit down, missing every shard of porcelain. She looked around and sighed. "There's no telling how old that set was."

"Old."

Juniper snorted at Tori's short answer. "At least my favorite cup is still at the police station, so it didn't get smashed. Do you think Beatrice will turn over a new leaf now, Tortellini?"

Tori frowned and tucked her hair behind her ear. "I'll believe it when I see it."

Garrett returned with the cleaning implements. "I put the cats in the front room," he said. "Luna and Finn were trying to follow me in here, and I didn't want them to get cut."

"Thanks, Garrett," Juniper said. She got up to take the broom, which he refused to hand over.

"Let me do this, June."

"All right, fine. But you better not be cleaning up because you think I can't handle it."

Garrett snorted. "Ha! Not likely. I just want to."

"Mm-hmm," Juniper grumbled, sinking back down in her chair, only to jump back up a second later. "Wait! Don't sweep it all up yet. This calls for a song."

Garrett shared a questioning look with Tori, and Tori shrugged, indicating she didn't have any more of a clue than he did as to what Juniper was doing.

Juniper hurried to the music hub she'd had specially installed in the central part of the mansion when she moved in. As a lover of music, she wanted to be able to hear it wherever she happened to be instead of missing it because she might have to leave the room.

She quickly swiped through her digital collection of songs until she got to the one she wanted to play. Then, with an almost maniacal grin on her face, she pressed Play.

"Another One Bites the Dust" filled the mansion, the heavy bass following her all the way back to the tea room, where Tori and Garrett stared at her with differing expressions on their faces, both of which meant *unbelievable*.

Never let it be said that Juniper Holiday was not prepared for any situation, no matter how dark. Cackling, she danced her way across the room, careful not to step on the broken porcelain, the black tourmaline at her pinky glinting in the overhead light.

CHAPTER TWENTY

*W*ith the mystery of the poisoning solved, Juniper was once again free to focus on what she loved best—besides Tori, of course—planning her own Holiday Christmas party (because Christmas was the next celebration day, and Juni always took advantage of those calendar events). But this one would (hopefully) not include a poisoning death.

"Should I invite the Duckman, Tori?" she called to the other room from her desk in the library.

"Sure, but he might not come. After dying at Thanksgiving, he might be a bit reluctant to dine with us... ever again," she finished, though more quietly.

Juniper's pen hovered over the page momentarily while she considered not inviting him. In the end, she waved the pen around a second, then said, "Oh, heck. I'm still inviting him."

"You can't try to make him play Santa, either," Tori cautioned, again from the other room.

Juniper frowned. "Whyever not? Oh, because he wouldn't know 'jolly' if it bit him in the—"

"June. Be nice."

Juniper sighed. "Aren't I always nice? I mean, really, I think I am. I bring you steak when I swing by Rarely Done. Coffee when I can't resist a WitchRoast cuppa. Hot buttered croissants—the ones you love—from the Dusty Buns Bakery when my sweet tooth kicks up, and we both know how often that is."

"So you bribe me for affection with foods you know I can't resist?" Tori asked, only this time her voice was much closer.

Juniper looked up to find her standing in the doorway, one ankle crossed over the other, her arms crossed over her middle as well. But she was smiling—a loving kind of smile. One that said she'd heard the words Juniper hadn't said as well as the ones she had. "I do love you, Juniper Holiday. You're the sweetest, silliest, most ridiculous, food-bribing, foulmouthed, crazy-dancing, loud-music-loving godmother a girl could have. I'd never trade you for another."

Juniper's eyes misted. "Aww, thanks."

"You know, I feel sort of bad for Beatrice. Do you think she'll keep her promise about not calling the cops on us?" Tori asked.

"I hope so. But I sort of feel bad for Poppy too. I mean, who could blame her for wanting to get rid of Beatrice?"

"Juniper!" Tori admonished. "There are better ways to get away from someone."

"True. At least my staff loves me. I don't have to worry about them trying to do away with me. Heck, they even stick around long after they are dead!" Juniper smiled at Jacobi, Felicity, and Lionel, who were floating in the corner.

Tori laughed. "If you say so. Anyway, at least everything turned out okay, and no one died."

Juniper simply nodded. Technically, Desmond had died, but she wasn't going to get too picky about it. "Let's hope we can keep it that way for the Christmas celebration. I don't need another party ruined by a murder, attempted or otherwise."

****

*C*hristmas season barely gets started when there's another murder at the Holiday mansion in the next book in the series - *Who Slayed The Santas?*

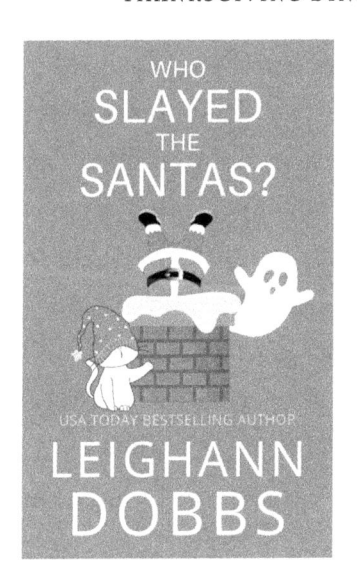

Excerpt From Who Slayed The Santas:

Felicity floated along the halls, a serene smile on her face. It was the wee hours of the morning and everyone was asleep. People wouldn't start rising for at least a half hour. The mansion was quiet, and she had the halls to herself.

Christmas at the Holiday mansion was always one of her favorite times. Back when she was alive, she loved putting up the decorations and directing the other servants in putting up the tree. Nowadays, she couldn't exactly do that. Her fingers always slipped right through the baubles, no matter how hard she concentrated on picking them up, and no one besides her fellow ghosts and Juniper could hear her anymore. Well, there was the detective now, too, but she could hardly bring herself to look him in the eye, much less speak to him. He was far too handsome.

Ah, well. She made herself content with the fact that she was still able to roam the beloved halls of the home that held so many warm holiday memories. Felicity had been around to see the mansion decorated by Juniper's ancestors. She'd seen the trees trimmed with real candles. She was glad those days were over and none of them had caused a fire. She'd also been around during the gaudy times of tinsel trees and one year the mistress had insisted on a pink artificial tree. Juniper liked real trees, and the taller the better. Felicity was glad since that's what she preferred, too.

Anna, Juniper's living housekeeper, did a splendid job with the decorations, and her command of the other living servants was spot on. Felicity liked to think that were she still alive, they would be fast friends. Anna kind of reminded her of her sister, Margaret, in her kindness and fortitude. But unlike Felicity, Margaret had moved on when she died, leaving her sister behind.

Christmas had been Maggie's favorite holiday. Had Maggie managed to stick around after her death, Felicity was sure she would love Juniper as well. Why Maggie had moved on, and Felicity had not, was a mystery. Why did some ghosts blip into the afterlife right away and others like herself, Lionel and Jacobi, linger here on earth? She had no idea. She didn't mind, though. She quite liked her life—or should she say death—here at the mansion. What was beyond was unknown, and she was in no hurry to get there. Though she did miss Maggie.

She gave a ghostly shake of her head to dispel that train of thought, for it often led to melancholy, and focused instead on her initial goal, which was double checking that Anna hadn't forgotten to put the train under the tree in the front parlor.

She floated down the hall, peeking into the

library to make sure the garland was draped on every shelf. Then she checked the west parlor to make sure the antique ivory nativity set was setup, and the stockings were hung from the mantel properly. Then on to the billiard room to see the velveteen reindeer display.

Everything was in perfect order, so she made her way to the front parlor. It was her favorite room! The tree must have been ten feet tall and decorated to perfection. The room was loaded with mistletoe, garland and lights. The cranberry and gold velvet skirt was spread under the tree and the train track ran around the edge.

But... why was the train stopped?

She wondered what the man slumped on the floor thought of it... wait a minute.

"Oh, dear," she muttered, hurrying to his side. "Are you all right?" she asked, hoping against hope that he would be another who could hear her. Alas, it was not to be. Fiddling with her fingers, she debated what she should do. She couldn't check him for a pulse. Her hand would simply slip right through.

Maybe she could get Jacobi, or even Lionel, to help her. No, that would take too long. There was no telling where either of them were currently, whereas she was right here. If the man needed help, he needed it right away. There was really only one thing to do about it, much as she didn't want to.

Grimacing, Felicity sank into his body, temporarily possessing him, only to jump out a moment later, shivers racing up and down her spine.

"Oh, you poor thing," she said, staring down at him sadly.

There was no getting around it. Santa Claus was dead.

MORE BOOKS BY LEIGHANN DOBBS:

Cozy Mysteries

Juniper Holiday Cozy Mysteries
***
Halloween Party Murder
Thanksgiving Dinner Death
Who Slayed The Santas?

Mystic Notch
Cat Cozy Mystery Series
* * *
Ghostly Paws
A Spirited Tail
A Mew To A Kill

MORE BOOKS BY LEIGHANN DOBBS:

Paws and Effect
Probable Paws
A Whisker of a Doubt
Wrong Side of the Claw
Claw and Order

Oyster Cove Guesthouse Cat Cozy Mystery Series
***
A Twist in the Tail
A Whisker in the Dark
A Purrfect Alibi

Moorecliff Manor Cat Cozy Mystery Series
* * *
Dead in the Dining Room
Stabbed in the Solarium
Homicide in the Hydrangeas
Lifeless in the Library

Silver Hollow

MORE BOOKS BY LEIGHANN DOBBS:

Paranormal Cozy Mystery Series

***

A Spell of Trouble (Book 1)
Spell Disaster (Book 2)
Nothing to Croak About (Book 3)
Cry Wolf (Book 4)
Shear Magic (Book 5)

Blackmoore Sisters Cozy Mystery Series

***

Dead Wrong
Dead & Buried
Dead Tide
Buried Secrets
Deadly Intentions
A Grave Mistake
Spell Found
Fatal Fortune
Hidden Secrets

Kate Diamond Mystery Adventures

MORE BOOKS BY LEIGHANN DOBBS:

***

Hidden Agemda (Book 1)
Ancient Hiss Story (Book 2)
Heist Society (Book 3)

Mooseamuck Island Cozy Mystery Series

* * *

A Zen For Murder
A Crabby Killer
A Treacherous Treasure

Lexy Baker Cozy Mystery Series

* * *

Lexy Baker Cozy Mystery Series Boxed Set Vol 1 (Books 1-4)

Or buy the books separately:

Killer Cupcakes
Dying For Danish
Murder, Money and Marzipan

MORE BOOKS BY LEIGHANN DOBBS:

3 Bodies and a Biscotti
Brownies, Bodies & Bad Guys
Bake, Battle & Roll
Wedded Blintz
Scones, Skulls & Scams
Ice Cream Murder
Mummified Meringues
Brutal Brulee (Novella)
No Scone Unturned
Cream Puff Killer
Never Say Pie

Lady Katherine Regency Mysteries
***

An Invitation to Murder (Book 1)
The Baffling Burglaries of Bath (Book 2)
Murder at the Ice Ball (Book 3)
A Murderous Affair (Book 4)
Murder on Charles Street (Book 5)

Hazel Martin Historical Mystery Series
***

Murder at Lowry House (book 1)
Murder by Misunderstanding (book 2)

MORE BOOKS BY LEIGHANN DOBBS:

Sam Mason Mysteries (As L. A. Dobbs)
***

Telling Lies (Book 1)
Keeping Secrets (Book 2)
Exposing Truths (Book 3)
Betraying Trust (Book 4)
Killing Dreams (Book 5)

Romantic Comedy
***
Corporate Chaos Series

In Over Her Head (book 1)
Can't Stand the Heat (book 2)
What Goes Around Comes Around (book 3)
Careful What You Wish For (4)

Contemporary Romance
***
Reluctant Romance

MORE BOOKS BY LEIGHANN DOBBS:

Sweet Romance (Written As Annie Dobbs)

Firefly Inn Series

***

Another Chance (Book 1)

Another Wish (Book 2)

Hometown Hearts Series

***

No Getting Over You (Book 1)

A Change of Heart (Book 2)

Sweet Mountain Billionaires

***

Jaded Billionaire (Book 1)

A Billion Reasons Not To Fall In Love (Book 2)

Regency Romance

* * *

Scandals and Spies Series:

MORE BOOKS BY LEIGHANN DOBBS:

Kissing The Enemy
Deceiving the Duke
Tempting the Rival
Charming the Spy
Pursuing the Traitor
Captivating the Captain

ABOUT THE AUTHOR

USA Today best-selling Author, Leighann Dobbs, has had a passion for reading since she was old enough to hold a book, but she didn't put pen to paper until much later in life. After a twenty-year career as a software engineer, with a few side trips into selling antiques and making jewelry, she realized you can't make a living reading books, so she tried her hand at writing them and discovered she had a passion for that, too! She lives in New Hampshire with her husband, Bruce, their trusty Chihuahua mix, Mojo, and beautiful rescue cat, Kitty.

Find out about her latest books by signing up at:
   https://leighanndobbscozymysteries.gr8.com

If you want to receive a text message alert on your cell phone for new releases , text

COZYMYSTERY to (603) 709-2906 (sorry, this only works for US cell phones!)

Connect with Leighann on Facebook
http://facebook.com/leighanndobbsbooks

This is a work of fiction.

None of it is real. All names, places, and events are products of the author's imagination. Any resemblance to real names, places, or events are purely coincidental, and should not be construed as being real.

THANKSGIVING DINNER DEATH

Copyright © 2022

Leighann Dobbs Publishing

http://www.leighanndobbs.com

All Rights Reserved.

No part of this work may be used or reproduced in any manner, except as allowable under "fair use," without the express written permission of the author.

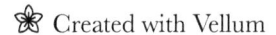

✼ Created with Vellum

Printed in the USA
CPSIA information can be obtained
at www.ICGtesting.com
LVHW010746251023
762064LV00034B/301